120 DAYS BOOKS

NEIL J. WESTON

NAKED
BOOK ONE
LAUNCH

CLASSIC QUEER PULP FICTION

Naked Launch: Book One by Neil J. Weston (edited by Maitland McDonagh) © 2018 120 Days

For more information contact:
Riverdale Avenue Books/120 Days
5676 Riverdale Avenue
Riverdale, NY 10471

www.riverdaleavebooks.com

Design by www.formatting4U.com
Cover by Scott Carpenter
Digital ISBN: 9781626014602
Print ISBN: 9781626014619
First Edition May 2018

Introduction

Gay Pirates of the Caribbean

Who *didn't* take one look at Johnny Depp's Captain Jack Sparrow—the flouncing, the eye shadow, the general peacockery and the coy finger to chin—and think, *"So* gay," especially considering he was the anchor character (if you'll pardon the nautical pun) of a major Disney franchise? And yet Depp's instincts and attitude—he said in 2015 he had told nervous studio executives that *all* his characters were gay— were vindicated and then some.

Neil J. Weston's epic *Naked Launch: Book One* (1968) and its equally lusty sequel, *Naked Launch: Book Two* (1969) is all over the idea that pirate ships were hotbeds of man love, and while historians could hardly be said to be in consensus, it makes considerable intuitive sense that, at the very least, seagoing men engaged in a good deal of situational same-sex activity and that some of it may well have been more than making the best of what was available.

To be fair, it's hard to accurately judge 17th-century attitudes about sexuality, in part because the mainstream historical record is generally hetero-normative, a notion so deeply inscribed in the thinking of certain eras that it was rarely, if ever, called into question. Yet anyone who's visited the portrait galleries of major museums, in person or online, can't help but see that the notion of what constitutes a "manly man" is far from fixed. In 17th-century portraits, silk breeches and kitten heels don't denote femininity, nor do ruffles, powdered wigs, fancy gloves, lace collars, flowing locks, full lips, manicured hands or makeup. Male beauty and vanity are celebrated in images bursting with pride in shapely legs, slim waists, liquid eyes and graceful hands.

The very existence of the French word *mateolage*—literally meaning "seamanship" but denoting a partnership between two buccaneers that, in the event of one man's death, allowed the other to inherit his property—is food for thought... perhaps with The Village People's 1979 "In the Navy" playing in the background ("where can you find pleasure/search the world for treasure"). So, too, is the fact that societal notions of masculinity are inconsistent across eras and cultures and that, as novelist L.P. Hartley famously observed, "[t]he past is a foreign country; they do things differently there" (*The Go-Between*, 1953). Or not, as the case may be.

Our protagonist Alan Steele—a porn star name if ever there was one—is a restless, middle-class youth who dreams of adventure and of making his fortune on the high seas. He indentures himself in return for passage on a ship headed to Jamaica—in essence selling himself into seven years of slavery, shipboard and on tropical plantations, for the promise that when he's done his time he'll again be free and still young enough to make his mark on the world.

Departing from Bristol, England, he befriends two other youths with similar ambitions: the practical Henry and dreamy, stoic Malcolm, with whom Alan falls deeply in love. All three discover that the old saying about sailing traditions being defined by rum, sodomy and the lash (famously attributed to Winston Churchill apropos the British Royal Navy, though there appears to be some question about the attribution's accuracy) is on the nose... or rather, on the backs and backsides of *Naked Launch*'s tender young men, who have no real idea what they've signed on for until it's too late. Backing out isn't an option—where are they to go when they're surrounded by merciless water?—and when they reach the Caribbean all three are sold off separately and Alan spends the next decade-and-a-half bulking up, toughening his hide through relentless flogging, and clinging to hope of somehow finding Malcolm, even as he exercises his "pego" (an oddly charming synonym for "prick" that appears to derive from Catalan/Spanish verbs meaning "to strike") as though he were preparing for the 17th-century Sex Olympics.

For all the novel's erotic acrobatics, *Naked Launch* is a vigorously old-fashioned mix of historical adventuring and unabashed romance. Alan matures from a callow youth into a scarred and toughened man, but remains a romantic to the core; he pines for Malcolm and develops serious relationships with several men. His heart may belong to his lost love, but he lives in a world in which death by disease and violence are common, in which devoted companions may be torn apart by sale, revolt and happenstance, and where the comfort of another man's arms can be the difference between killing despair and holding fast to the resolution to keep on living.

Author Weston clearly steeped himself in nautical lore, peppering the novel with guest appearances by notorious real-life pirates, buccaneers and privateers, of whom my favorite is Captain Morgan, immortalized in the 20th and 21st centuries by the annexation of his name to the popular spiced rum. (Here I must note the recipe for the "Flaming Gay Morgan": Captain Morgan spiced rum, cherry liqueur, tonic water and a dash of Bacardi, served alight).

But Weston also brings a distinctly contemporary perspective to his story of men, ships and whips. While PTSD—post-traumatic stress disorder—lacked a name until 1980, it's clear that Alan is defined by it. He's been systematically brutalized and denied acknowledgement of his fundamental humanity so long that down looks like up. And yet Alan sustains a core belief that love matters and, in a broader sense, that the ability to feel a deep emotional connection with another person—not just visceral lust—is what makes him human, even when he's being treated, at best, like a beast of burden.

Weston also brings to the mix a distinctly personal fetish (though by no means outré) regarding the hirsute and the hairless. The young Alan is defined by his lush pelt of body hair, signifying his masculine nature. But when a tropical fever leaves Alan denuded, as bare as a newborn babe, Weston turns to a celebration of ultimate nudity. Robbed of every vestige of his rude ursine beauty, Alan becomes an exotic, stripped to his most naked essence—nothing stands between him and the touch of various lovers.

Alan's overt and hard-won masculinity—by the end of *Naked Launch*, no one would ever mistake him for a callow youth—combined with his eerie nakedness make him a distinctive protagonist in a literary era characterized by two extremes: the twink and the macho man.

Naked Launch is a period novel, but its concerns remain strikingly modern: What does it mean to be a man, specifically a gay man in a largely straight culture? How do individuals find places for themselves within largely hostile mainstream cultures? And what is love worth when laws and conventions trend in a different direction? *Naked Launch* comes down firmly on the side of love, arguing through the conventions of gay adult pulp fiction that love has everything to do with it, and that to deny one's own nature is to deny life itself. It also embraces a particular notion of masculinity whose cornerstones are tough and hairy— oh, so very hairy. Though a skinny, smooth-skinned youth when the novel opens, Alan matures into a robust, muscular man whose luxurious pelt excites women and men alike, though Alan, of course, has no interest in the ladies who cast admiring glances his hirsute way.

Gay adult novels of the 1960s and '70s were by no means political manifestos; they were first and foremost entertainments, erotic books aimed at a large but underserved audience of gay men looking for sexually explicit amusement. But at its best, the gay adult publishing industry provided an outlet for writers who wanted to create accessible, popular fiction— often crafted within the parameters of pulp genre conventions—built around gay characters navigating their lives and loves in their own way, despite the hostility that eventually prompted the Stonewall riots and launched an era of gay-rights activism. Simply by existing, novels like *Naked Launch*, which use pulp conventions to explore the lives of gay men in full, played their own part in that revolution and managed to be enormously entertaining as well.

—Maitland McDonagh,
Editor, 120 Days Books

Chapter One

Alan Steele lustily proclaimed his entry into a world of insecurity to be wholly against his will. This was looked upon by the midwife as a sign he would become a great man and she ignored his protests while she deftly tied the knot. Seven months later, happening to visit while he was about to be bathed, she gave a toothless smile and exclaimed, "Fain be it, if his pego be so stiff and grows with him, he'll not have need to challenge men; he will beckon and they will follow!" She nodded her head gravely, certain of her prediction.

The family that came to have the surname "Steele" had a discrete and modest beginning some 60-odd years before the birth of Alan, around 1570, a wondrous feat brought about by none other than Sir Walter Raleigh and one of the Queen's maids of honor. They chanced one day to meet in a remote corner of the palace garden where Sir Walter had sought relief behind a tree. So absorbed had he been in flipping about his gratifying appendage to create a pattern on the bark that he had not heard her approach. He made no compromise, releasing the last of his golden stream, grateful because she had frozen in her steps. At the end he stepped back and, with no wasted motion in his gallant fashion, swept off his plumed hat with one hand, extended his cape with the other, made a foot to her and bowed from his waist.

"If it please you, fair mistress," he said with smooth courtesy, but also a slight frown: In his haste to display his gentlemanly air he had not completed his handiwork and those inevitable last drops were now staining the fine satin of his pantaloons. He wished strongly she would oblige him quickly and release him from the strained position so he could shake out the last of it and end his dripping.

"My lord," she said demurely as she turned down her head in proper fashion, lifted her skirts slightly and curtsied, "'tis my pleasure."

The sight of the trim ankles exposed under the skirts turned the pleasure into a flood in Sir Walter's mind. As he brought his body upright, he evidenced his delight in a hastening erection. The maid, seeing the plum-like tip emerging, cried out and stumbled, her back pressing against the tree. Modesty was upright in her mind and she drew up her skirts to shield her face. Sir Walter—always a man of action upon seeing a damsel in distress—cast his cape to the ground and sought to console her.

"What do you ask me?" she cried as he began boarding her, then, "Will you undo me?" Her fear seemed not great, for she hitched the skirts even higher when he did not answer, he being so occupied in setting the plum to the ruby lips. Sir Walter, finding such accommodation with the skirts, urged them higher, the better to view his solid, throbbing flesh make its long journey into her. And when that was done he caught her hips firmly and gloried in the distance he had to swing his buttocks to heat and ripen the plum. Each long traverse hardened the rod further, setting the veins to bulging. Inside his pantaloons, his purse of balls lessened their swinging as his passion mounted. "Nay, sweet Sir Walter," she cried. "Sweet Sir Walter! Sir Walter!" Each cry seemed weaker and the quiver in her voice greater as she caught his spirit and began crying out with ecstasy, setting her hips gyrating.

The compounded motion set Sir Walter's vitals aflame and he gave a lusty thrust that buried the burdened stem well within her. For a moment he felt suspended, floating, while his mind's eye saw that tip blossom into fullness and become dark like the choicest of purple plums, shiny of skin and filled with sweet essence. Moments later, ever so weak and gasping for breath as he withdrew, he was certain he had thoroughly inundated every inner recess.

The maid, still quivering, was not certain of anything but that she would swoon and she lowered her skirts slowly. Before her, again, was the gentleman in full curtsy, with foot extended and bowing at the waist. Her training prompted immediate response with a curtsy, but then she caught sight of the enormous plum, streaked with the excess and still throbbing, so she swooned instead.

Month later, when her burden was well upon her and the pleasures which began it were nearly forgotten, she went stomping about declaring, "I swear upon my honor he did steal and fill me with child upon which he will not put his name!" Then in a moment of inspiration she proclaimed, "The child will have a proper name and 'twill be Walter Dide Steale!" Raleigh, rather than find anger in this accusative name, found amusement and set up a fine manor for them.

In time, Walter Steale developed apprehensions and artfully respelled the name, so it became "Steele." This was almost of no consequence, for he sired a family of 11 daughters and only one son, whom he named Roger Steele. His opportunities to further insure the name were limited, for he met his demise from a pistol in the hands of an irate husband while involved in a game of cuckoldry.

Roger Steele maintained the traditions of his forebears. Of his legitimate children there were four daughters and one son. Unlike his father, he lacked the perseverance to learn whether she might produce more—he played far afield and reached the conclusion that it was her fault, as all others bore only males for him. His untimely fate came only moments after taking one young maid's honor, whereupon she had the indiscretion to cry out loudly of her pleasure when her father was within earshot. Without regard for that trying moment when the ball from the pistol created a gaping wound in his chest, he plunged his shaft deeply and thrilled as he begat another son.

William Steele, the son of Roger, set no procreative records after his marriage. He was highly devoted to the manor, it seemed, and raised it from the neglect into which it had fallen. William's constant presence there was due to the fact that he had been kicked by a horse in a manner that throttled his fertility without impeding his prowess. His pleasures came to him in the form of maids and wives who took to hiding in the stable to pounce upon him for a roll in the hay, knowing of their safety in so doing. Word of his capability—or lack of it—spread, along with distorted reports of enormity. Soon curious youths numbered among his visitors and William enjoyed greater variety in his pleasure.

By the time Alan, William's only son, achieved his maturity, he had observed a great many things that fueled his desires. One warm day he had climbed a tree in the orchard to seek a breeze. The pressure against branches, the moisture of perspiration and the roughness of his breeches combined to tease up an attention-centering erection with the need for vigorous exercise. He dropped to the ground and hurried his steps to seek the intimacy of his bedchamber.

Alan never reached the room, for he caught sight of a youth furtively stealing into the stable. Thinking the young man was up to no good, Alan hastened there only to hear his father's voice from within. Curiosity prompted him to enter unobserved and take a station at one of the stalls, since from this vantage point he could see beyond the pile of hay without being observed.

Alan's nerves were soon set to tingling and he reached into the slit of his breeches; the game he observed excited the inner reaches of his imagination and brought on him a rigidity beyond all previous experience. The youth's mouth was fully filled by Sir William, who had both hands clasped behind the lad's head. Under William's encouragement, the youth took to flaying his own stiff cock and Alan attended to his own throbbing erection. William's buttocks were clenched and the youth's shoulders shaking violently as Alan beheld the unbelievable sight of the white burst that issued from the youth's member.

Their gasps covered the sounds of Alan's escape. He had not a chance of going very far with that unbendable rod sticking out of his breeches, so he dashed behind the stable while clawing at the fabric to pull it free from under his belt. Free of breeches, Alan wrapped his fingers about the tool and was soon writhing and gasping while flinging far and wide. Alan took to hiding in the stable for many weeks after that and observed the full gamut, continuing to extract his pleasure. Coincidental with this was a turn of mind. Alan's father was of the old generation, content with work at the manor, bettering their way of living and accumulating wealth. But Alan was of the new generation: There were lands to be conquered, spoils to be won and wars to be fought. He was not willing to sit back and restrict his living to ordinary existence.

Although Alan had not taken very well to tutoring, his reading ability was considerable and he could not get enough books to satisfy him. Systematically, he exhausted the collection put at his disposal by the minister of their church at Buckinghamshire. It took a full year and set his mind to daydreams about the intriguing West Indies.

Alan was 18 and a few months the afternoon he informed his mother he was on the way to return some books to the minister and would be a while.

"It forebodes a long while," she said, commenting about the strength of the hug he gave her.

"'Tis to be," said Alan, holding some misgivings about the rush of affection he had displayed. "'Tis not to worry if I do not return in time for supper. 'Tis old enough I am to take care of myself."

"That you are, Alan my son." She chewed on her inner cheek with some anxiety and then said, "Well, give my regards to them. Be sure to thank them if you take supper at their home."

Alan rushed out of the house, his eyes moist, as he least expected they would be. He turned to the orchard, hoping his father would understand his lack of farewell, the better to enjoy the wench who was stealing into the stable. In the orchard, he recovered his cape, with food and other items wrapped in a large kerchief, the lot hidden earlier that day. Without creating any suspicion, he supped with the minister and family and took his departure, explaining that he would not borrow any books because other matters would occupy him. At the crossroad, he turned into the one which would eventually lead him to ships.

Although weary and footsore, Alan Steele was wide-eyed with excitement from the moment he caught his first glimpse of the activity at the docks in Bristol. The smell of tar and salt, mingled with those of fish, of spices and of tea, became an elixir. The sound of water slapping against the sides of ships, the severity of commands, the harsh swearing… all were like the finest music. He set foot on the quay and begin walking, seeing so much of what he had read become a reality. Seamen did walk with that swaggering clumsy sea walk; they were burly fellows; they did wear loops in their ears; they did pull back their hair to be held in place by tarred pigtails, while that on their faces—if there were no smooth chin—formed whiskers curled in ringlets. One lad, who looked even younger than Alan, stopped his diligent swabbing of a deck to wave. Alan dropped his bundle to wave back. There was a friendliness here, a kinship which he liked.

Where William Steele had taken great pains to instruct his sons in exercise, his intentions had not been general. Alan Steele was an odd sight on that quay. He was a tall, gangling youth, as narrow at his shoulders as at his waist and hips. His head seemed large against these proportions and yes, if it were carried on a developed body, it would cause others to take notice. There was a handsome face below the tousle of lush black hair, with keen eyes scanning under heavy black brows which ran straight before sweeping into shapely arches. His nose was fine and straight, slightly tanned, but looked pale next to the bloom on his cheeks. His mouth was always open, as if ever on the verge of becoming a warm smile, showing enough of the sound white teeth between the full lips. His chin contradicted the deception given by his mouth, being nearly square and almost with a cleft, marking the will and determination his character bore. Alan Steele was handsome of face and much too fine an individual to be found as a messmate aboard a ship or to be wandering along the quay. Two hands from a merchant command thought so too, and they blocked his path.

"What have we here?" said the short one, exaggerating a look of surprise. "A ship's lad, I'd say, and fine one, too."

Alan, still starry eyed, was barely able to take his eyes from their stare at the man's earlobe, where the loop had stretched the hole to let the ring swing freely. He forced his attention to the other man who was saying "Aye, mate. Would you be telling us what vessel you're with?"

Alan felt please to find they did not consider him to be a landsman. "I have to find my ship," he told them. "I have not yet been to sea."

"And here 'twas thought he had the smack of the sea about him," exclaimed the short one

"Aye," agreed the other, "and where would you be bound?"

"To the West Indies, if you please. I have read much about them, and 'tis there I shall seek my riches."

"Polite he is and has some learning," said the short one. "A young man should be looking to his future, I says. And on what vessel were you planning to purchase passage?"

Alan's teeth glistened brightly as he formed a full smile. "I have barely a shilling and a few groat. I shall work my passage."

Both men look at each other with horror. "Aye, dearie me, I say," proclaimed the short one. "I would not have been so brave in my youth!" The other was shaking his head with wonderment. "Nor me!"

"'Tis a good hand I shall be, and I learn rapidly. I might even become a man before the mast on the first voyage and be worthy of my passage."

Now the short one took to shaking his head. "If you live long enough!" His eyes showed compassion and he kept shaking his head. "As you will be the youngest one aboard, and 'tis their due to have a daily flogging for the amusement of the crew, may you bear it well. Then, when you come to shore, the captain will have to cover your costs of passage and he will sell you to a plantation. Such a debt to your new owner will require you to work for him as an indentured man."

Alan's eyes kept flicking from one face to the other. The seamen look so serious and sad, it seemed they were truthful. "But I will have worked my passage," he pointed out.

"Aye," agreed the second man, "that you will, between the floggings and the hard labor you will be put to, not to speak of the sore bum from serving the crew who long for a fair wench. But 'tis always these youths with the sea in their eyes who bear the pains of the voyage and are then sold into slavery."

His words sounded ominous, yet he winked at the short one. "'Tis good we came about to speak with you."

"Aye, mate. Now lad, what say we fix it with our bos'n and you sails with us? I takes a liking to you, and we could fix it so's you be free when we arrive. What say you?"

There was little Alan had read about indentured men, usually men taken from prisons. He had never read about the practice of flogging the youngest youth, but the words coming from experienced men had a ring of truth to them. He needed protection and readily agreed.

"Then it's fixed, as good as a piece of eight. Now, to take care of the fixing, we must now know that you *do* have the money."

Reluctantly, Alan brought out his shilling and four groat. They were scooped up from his barely opened palm, and the men immediately set to leaving.

"The bos'n may be having a bribe, you know. Fear not—board our vessel and let the bos'n know we sent you to wait for us."

As the men merged with another lot of happy seamen, Alan lost his desire to pursue them and plead for a few groat to cover a meal. When he thought it through, he realized he would be eating onboard in only a few hours and it was not that important. With cape thrown over his shoulder, he assumed a swaggering tread while he whistled softly. There was still a great deal to be seen along this quay and, undoubtedly, more exciting things. He was at the midpoint, storing away in his memory the exotic names of vessels when he realized he did not know what ship the men had come from or what their names were. He soon realized too that he had been fleeced.

Chapter Two

A sad, more worldly and very hungry Alan leaned against a pile of sacks and watched the youth wielding his knife with skill through a loaf of bread. Like a caress, Alan's fingers were passing over and over the word "Barbados" inscribed on the sack where his arm rested. Without a doubt, there was rich brown sugar inside, but there was no rent, not the slightest hole through which some of the sweetness would trickle to give him sustenance. As the other youth ripped off goodly chunk of bread with his teeth and then brought up a piece of cheese, Alan could not help licking his lips. If he had not been so foolish, he could have had the same, many times over… the bite he expected on the cheese was long overdue. He looked up at dark eyes staring at him.

"Have you no food?"

Alan lowered his eyes, unwilling to admit that he who had never lacked anything now lacked everything.

As much as he wanted to nod his head, his hunger made him shake it.

"Well, come along. I have enough for two."

Alan had no hesitancy to respond and he was soon seated next to the other lad, transfixed in his stare at the large piece of bread being cut for him. Bread had never had a finer flavor, he decided, as he chewed happily on his first bite; better would be that piece of cheese offered to him. His mouth was much too full to offer his thanks and he shyly looked at the other youth, hoping his eyes told what his heart felt.

The other, Henry, smiled pleasantly, hardly any upper lip showing, it being thin. His eyes showed an inner warmth, set deep because of the high cheekbones. Like Alan, Henry also had black hair, but his was wiry, coiled like springs against his head. His body was compact, of good stock but still carrying some of the childhood fat. In the matter of young people judging another of the same age, Alan new he had found a friend.

Henry had come from the estate of Llanrhymney in Glamorganshire. His Welsh background showed in the rich, rolling laugh he produced when Alan told him of his misfortune.

"I fare much better, Alan," Henry said with a nod of his head, still laughing. "I have bought me a way to the West Indies; I want none of this slavery, nor do I wish to be flogged."

"I ran away with no money. It needs be I must work my way and take my floggings, if that is my due. So much money is beyond me."

"'Tis only four guineas it took, Alan. You are mistaken if you think I go as a passenger; I took up with a bos'n, George Harvey by name, and bought him some ales in a tavern. A good man he is. The vessel goes to Barbados and he will smuggle me ashore."

"Even a few guineas is a fortune to me," Alan sighed with resignation. "'Tis indenture for me. The seven years will pass rapidly enough and I shall still be young enough to seek fortunes."

Henry could not see this course of action. He counted up what money he had and scratched his head long and hard.

"If I bribe Harvey with an equal amount, I can get you aboard and still have some left for our lodgings in Barbados."

Alan's eyes opened wide. His sincerity was honest when he declared, "Oh, Henry, I would give my greatest pledge to repay you immediately after, if you would do this for me."

With quick decision, Henry scrambled to his feet and was off to the tavern. Alan could feel his heart speaking heavily as he set about offering a prayer.

The sense of motion and the strange creaking, sounding harsh against the brush of water along the sides of the ship, set Alan's heart pounding an instant after he opened his eyes. It was dark in the hold where Harvey had hidden them among the many boxes and bales, but he could tell Henry was awake. He asked, to make sure.

"Maybe for an hour," said Henry, "since they first cast off the lines. 'Tis most exciting, this 15th day of June in 1651. One to remember!"

Neither he nor Alan were ever forget that day. The memory was implanted securely hours later when they heard Harvey's voice at the entrance to the hold. Two men came down after him.

"See that all is stowed safe! We want none of this shifting about in the storm," he ordered gruffly, while he set a lantern on a peg. "Be swift, for the cap'n will be anxious to have his services this Lord's Day. I'll see what lays forward."

Like his voice, his actions were rough and he knocked things about as he came near where the youths were hidden. Fearful, Alan reached out to find Henry's hand. Henry was just as frightened, showing it with a heavy grip. Harvey was nearly alongside when they heard the shift of a bale, one being pushed firmly. When it fell on Henry, he let out howl as the breath was knocked out of him.

"What's this? What's this?" Harvey called out, pulling the bail off Henry. "Cap'n Will have quite a surprise when he learns how big the rats have come to be in his hold."

Henry howled more while being yanked into the passage area and Allen scrambled far back for greater security.

"Here, take this one," Harvey called to the other two, "and get him on deck. 'Tis another here needs catching!"

On the deck, firmly held, Alan looked longingly at the shore, which still carried pockets of fog. Where green could be seen, no green had ever appeared greener to his eyes. Once clear of Bristol Channel, it would be a long time before a green not of the sea would beckon. He braced himself as the captain emerged from the cabin. Alan was certain a word of explanation of how they came aboard would reverse the bosun's position and if worst came about they could still be put ashore.

Alan never gained opportunity to implicate the bosun, being constantly reminded of his manners while the Captain spoke. At last the droned tirade was concluded with the captain ordering good care for the two, as they would bring the price of their passage on sale in Barbados.

Set free again, they had the last word from the bosun who threatened the heaviest of flogging if they dared hint of his involvement. They gave their word and were turned over to the cook, a kindly man, who filled them with the cold leftovers from the crew's breakfast. Alan did not much care for the stiff leg which caused the cook to hobble, but his attention in straightening Alan's mussed hair while he ate was pleasant and done with a light touch. He liked the man, he decided when they had to return to the deck to begin their training at sea.

It was inevitable that they were to share the ship's boy's chores and they joined him swabbing the decks. Their next bit of learning was of what a God fearing man was their captain. It was to be their obligation to stand with the crew for two hours on each Lord's Day and hear the captain's monotonous voice preach his sermons about the need for kindness between men and the dispatch of all evil.

It was late afternoon before they could meet up with the ship's boy, Malcolm, and bond a friendship. He was a bit younger than they and his eyes bothered Alan; as passive as they seemed, having a color brown so dark as to be almost black, there was something like the flames of a fire barely smoldering deep within them. Otherwise, he was very pleasing to look at and his strong body had the peculiarity of bending backwards at the hips with flexibilities where least expected. Allen sensed a greater partiality to Malcolm then to Henry, regardless of the fact that Henry had already tried to help him. Besides, Malcolm's lips were full of beckoning sensuality and they made his mouth look quite large.

16

Malcolm was the one who took them about the barque; he had been aboard for nearly a week and had gained familiarity with the ship. He also got together some things to make sleeping more comfortable in the forecastle with the rest of the crew. For the first night they slept together, close for extra warmth. Alan was the last to go to sleep, finding a strange pleasure in the nearby form of Malcolm. With unaccountable boldness, he stole his hand down to close it over the crotch of Malcolm's breeches. Nice as it was, his hand was taken from there and placed higher, about the chest. Alan was just as pleased to have it there; the voyage would be long. The last thought to race through his mind was that as stern as the captain seemed to be, his sermon showed that he was a kind man. "There must be kindness between men," he had said.

The scramble of the crew responding to the bosun's pipe set the lads to scrambling as well. The early dawn had a chill to it and a brisk wind filled the sails. Already feeling equal to the seamen, they had abandoned shoes. Underfoot they could feel the salt from the spray settling on the deck. There was a spume on the choppy water about them. The crew was divided along the bulwarks, facing the mainmast. Henry was to one side and Alan to the other. Malcolm was about to take a position aside Alan when the bosun's mate took hold of his arm and brought him before the mast. The captain emerged from his cabin.

"Henceforth," he announced, "in the custom of our vessels, the youngest member of the crew is to receive the lash—but laid lightly, mind you, bos'n. 'Tis to be a reminder to all hands that any infraction of the ship's rule or failure at duty will bring on a flogging that will *not* be laid on so lightly. For the ship's boy, 'tis to toughen his hide and nettle his spirit with lashing on each Monday. Proceed with a dozen!"

Alan felt weak while struggling with his will, which demanded he go to Malcolm's assistance. His eyes searched the faces of all the crew while the bosun's mate stripped off the singlet of the pale-faced youth before the mast. All hands were looking forward to this exhibition and Alan came to realize that none would side with him. He turned his back and faced the last sight of land. He would not watch this cruel, senseless flogging, especially now upon seeing how fine a body Malcolm had. Few youths had removed their shirts in his father's stable and none had so beautiful a chest. Alan pressed his crotch against the bulwark to squelch the peaking in his breeches which began the instant he pictured how Malcolm's nipples had stood prominently erect in the cold air. It was the captain's order that made him snap back to attention and turn about. Poor Malcolm was already tied to the mast and the bosun was uncoiling his whip.

The fire in Malcolm's eyes went beyond smoky to smoldering when they were taking their breakfast. "It could have been worse," he admitted. "My back may smart, but at least I was not cut." He winced as Alan thoughtlessly put his arm around him; compassion would have to be by words and not contact.

Alan was overly attentive to Malcolm through the day, except when he sneaked his way to the galley to beg for a treat that would offset Malcolm's ill feelings. Seeming to have anticipated this visit, the cook was most generous with special treats for Alan and the promise of more on future visits. His words lulled

Alan, who found no reason against having his breeches pulled down.

"Aye," said the cook with freshened look, "a finer pecker I have never seen. 'Tis one you could only cradle in your arms and rock; to my wits end, I would not know what else to do with it." Alan appreciated his admiration, showing it with a forward thrust of his hips. "Here lad, this deserves my treat of special sweet biscuits which not even to the captain I'll serve."

The delightful taste of the biscuits made Alan yielding and he was willing to rest on the chopping block to accommodate the locked knee of the cook. Although he had never experienced it, he knew what he was in for having seen youths squirm and cry under his father's coupling. The cook, however, was not greatly blessed and Alan could see there would be little suffering. Later, of all the crewmen he most appreciated the cook for his use of lard rather than the sticky pomade others had in their kits. It did not matter much, as long as the store of biscuits was in reach while he was over the block.

That night he was anxious to tell Malcolm of the good biscuits the cook had in the galley, but Malcolm avoided any contact, remaining face down. Alan was afraid to touch the sore back and, from the way Malcolm kept swallowing, Alan was certain he was sobbing.

Two mornings later, instead of receiving the day's orders as they had the day before, Alan found his arm caught by the bosun's mate. Alarm filled him when he was taken before the mast. When the captain appeared, he heard his doom.

"Those who would steal their passage must be taught the ways of right," droned the captain. "On each

Wednesday, for the remainder of the voyage, this young man is to receive his share of the lash, laid lightly, mind you bos'n. The other shall have his due each Friday: Proceed with a dozen!"

Alan was not as reticent as Malcolm had been and, as the bosun's mate stripped the singlet from him, he darted forward. The crew was not to be cheated of their amusement and caught him in short order, pinning him face down to the deck. Alan begged them to pull up the breeches that had slipped from under his belt during the commotion and promised he would relent to the whipping. Jeering, they flipped him over. Whistles and coarse remarks were sounded while they looked at his nakedness before lifting him to his feet. A cryptic request was thrown to the bosun just as his breeches were stripped off over his bare feet.

"Cap'n?" the bosun asked, after a long stare at Alan's possibilities.

"Do with him as you wish! He needs a severe lesson!" the captain snarled, turning on his heel to enter the cabin, dismissing all interest.

Moments later, Alan had to stop his squirming. He had been triced so that his limbs formed an "X," his legs widespread and his arms pulled high enough that he could only stand on the balls of his feet. With the rolling of the ship, it was as though the clapper of a bell were striking his inner thighs.

The bosun looked at Alan with a twisted smile as he calmly removed the last item from Alan's body, a wide strap of leather.

Harvey tested the end against his open palm, glanced at Alan's crotch and then improved his smile with a greater twist.

Alan glared at the bosun until the man had positioned himself behind and to the side, where Alan could not see. He looked quickly at all the faces to each side of him. There could be no help: All the faces leered with anticipation. He could not understand the expectancy they showed in lustful eyes. Even Malcolm could not be counted on: At this distance it was easy to see his eyes flame like torches while his tongue played over his lips.

It was not until the belt sounded a third crack across his buttocks that Alan realized the strange position and the contractions of the muscles in his legs, abdomen, groin and buttocks left him with no control against erection. To make matters worse, the bosun did not use evenly spaced strikes and he could not brace himself against the unexpected. The men cheered the bosun and complimented Alan for this magnificent treat. Helplessly, Alan tilted his head to view the grossness of his display and to see if he could exert his will. He became as fascinated as the crew; the strains and pressure had his cockhead bulging with a brilliant shine over the dark color and the shaft was distended with solidity like purple-veined marble. On the eighth crack, a long silvery thread dangled from the tip. On the 11th, the thread carried streaks of white and the cock bolted farther upward, now painfully rigid.

Alan's muscles ached far more from the leverage of that weighty head than from the strikes of the belt. On the 14th crack, a heavy white burst arced out to hit the deck nearly six feet ahead of him. Writhing was impossible under the tricing and each involuntary contraction of his buttocks threw bursts that brought on cheers from the crew. Alan was sure something had been broken in him to bring forth so much and, at last, while

21

hanging limply from his arms his body nearly vibrating from exhaustion, he continued to drip onto the deck.

The bosun, still wearing his twisted smile as he untied Alan, calmly informed him that since he had spoiled the deck he would have to swab it all before he could have breakfast, As the cords on his arms slacked, Alan found his legs would not support him; he allowed himself to be lowered until he sat hunched on the deck. It was Malcolm who rushed to him and began wiping away the white marks still be formed on his thigh. Alan began breathing easier, discovering that under Malcolm's hand a limpness was setting in. Malcolm stopped for an instant and gazed at him silently. The sensuous lips were only a scant distance away and Alan wanted to meet them, but Malcolm returned his attention to the softening cock, dabbing.

Henry proved to be the weakest, squealing like a pig each time the whip lay across his back. By the captain's order, this entitled him to six additional lashes, the last raising a heavy welt. These same six also disclosed Harvey's nature, for he smiled to the limit while he strengthened each of the last blows. After that Friday, Alan began receiving looks of admiration and winks from the crew, while Henry received only jests.

The boys performed their duties now while counting out the days before they would have to face the mast or be triced. Malcolm's eyes flashed angrily each time his singlet was stripped from him, but he refused to cry out as the bosun wished him to. On the fourth flogging, Harvey went heavy with the whip; Alan was sickened as blood began trickling down Malcolm's back. At the end of a dozen lashes, the bosun's mate carried the unconscious Malcolm to Harvey's quarters, as ordered.

Malcolm remained stubbornly quiet through the rest of the day, except when Alan was dressing his cuts. Alan thought at one point that he had hurt Malcolm, but the way Malcolm remained face down, pulled close to Alan with his arm about him said otherwise; the deluge of tears and rending sobs had been unleashed by love. Alan only wished that night that he could hold Malcolm tightly and kiss every part of his body without hurting the lacerated back. But he had to remain content with the attention he did receive. By Alan's reckoning, it was the first time Malcolm had closed his hand over Alan's and kept his hold through the night.

There was great excitement the next morning: The ship's master had been found with his throat neatly slit and the bloody knife was the bosun's. Traces of blood were also found on Harvey's breeches; it was a highly frightened man pleading innocence who was tied to the mast that day, and it was the glowering captain who took it upon himself to extract the punishment. Blood was drawn by the first stroke of the cat o' nine tails, and it continued falling heavily until the flesh on Harvey's back hung in tatters and the ribs showed. At the end, it was only a corpse shuddering under the additional blows. Still breathing heavily from the exertion, the captain proclaimed, "That shall be the end of flogging! None of you will ever forget this and reminders shall not be necessary. Now throw that bastard overboard and get him out of my sight. Only pray the master's mate knows his navigation well."

Malcolm was nearly smiling when the three boys were later able to speak, away from the crew. He said nothing when Henry said, "I thank the Lord for salvation from that man," but his eyes flamed. He did not answer directly when Henry said, "You would not speak yesterday. When the mate took you to Harvey's quarters, did he…?" He could not further develop the question; he could never speak of the act since that time when his squeals had been heard all over the ship after a crewman had taking a fancy to him.

There was a dark flash in Malcolm's eyes before he slowly nodded his head. "Like a madman, as 'twas not enough to take; he pushed and rubbed his dirty, hairy chest right in the blood on my back, he did."

Alan was watching carefully as Malcolm turned his eyes to the water and as much of a smile as he could produce began forming. Alan tried the question which had been forming in his mind. "Malcolm, did the bosun really kill the ship's master?"

Malcolm turned his head suddenly and their eyes locked. "'Twas his knife, was it not?" he asked quietly, while he pushed his way between Alan and Henry, then took to silence as he returned to his duties.

Throughout the day, Alan could not help noticing how uncomfortable Malcolm looked and how his breeches peaked. When Malcolm had to go into the hold for some supplies, Alan stole after him. He had to confirm what he could not believe. He confirmed Malcolm's erection, and while his hand closed on the breeches, Malcolm looked straight into Alan's eyes. His lips looked fuller and redder, and Alan sampled them. Then, when Malcolm leaned back from the hips most provocatively, Alan dropped to his knees, pulling down firmly on Malcolm's breeches. He wished they could remove all their clothes and be in the light of day: Malcolm's erect cock fully complemented the beautiful body and comely features.

Chapter Three

Severe treatment by "civilized" men was the rule rather than the exception during the 17th century, and Alan, Henry and Malcolm were among the fortunate ones to have suffered the least. The conditions around them, however, were to develop their natures at the most influential period of their lives. In Spain and its colonies, the Inquisition took its toll. In England and her colonies, the law inflicted unspeakable tortures upon criminals and malefactors for the most trivial offenses, penalties that included branding, hanging by thumbs, flogging and pillory, cutting off ears and hands and even the slitting of tongues. Legitimate everyday punishments even included impaling, quartering, flaying alive and hanging in chains. By this measure, for the good of man, the captain had inflicted a proper punishment on the bosun.

While flogging aboard the vessel had been stayed, it applied only to the former flogging of the ship's youngest. The unwieldy crew had to be kept in place and welting was relatively frequent. In an age when punishment and sex had no evil label and were freely indulged, the youths had little choice. Henry's constant squealing made him extremely unpopular, so Alan and Malcolm bore the brunt of it. Midway through the voyage, they no longer feared any of their messmates, having found their bores equal to any onslaught.

Nevertheless, years seemed to pass before the day when the cry from the masthead that Barbados had been sighted sent them rushing to the forecastle deck for their first glimpse of the West Indies. It was disappointing. The speck on the horizon barely offered a promise, yet throughout the day they glanced frequently toward it, wholly forgetting any sufferings they had experienced during the voyage. By the light of the midday sun details of the land were barely discernable, but there was no doubting that the greens of the island were so intense they looked almost blue. Their hearts pumped a new blood with a heavy beat as they tried to picture their future holdings of land, silver and gold. Then, when the anchor stopped its plunge and the sails were furled, exotic tropical scents replaced the tang of sea air and the smell of the ship. There were palms to be seen on shore, their fronds barely moving in the slight breeze, beckoning. The lads pitched anxiously into the work of making the vessel shipshape to hasten disembarking.

The hands, except for the ship's watch, had been gone for more than an hour while the youths were detained. Malcolm's patience was dwindling and he tried convincing Alan and Henry that they were not so far from shore as to be unable to gain it safely by swimming. Henry paled at the suggestion, for he did not know how to swim. Alan feared the wrath of the captain, insisting that shots would be fired upon them— the hazard was too great. Malcolm said he would go on his own and was about to climb the taffrail when the captain came on deck and ordered them to take positions near him. Soon the four small boats they had seen approaching bumped against the side of the ship. One of the men within did not even bother coming over the rail after glancing at them, giving a grunt of disgust and saying to the captain, "As bad as the last lot! I'll not be coming to see you again."

The others began pinching, shoving and pushing the youths to examine them. Malcolm was the first to be purchased: His temper had flared and he had shoved back; this spirit netted the captain eighteen pounds. Fear surged in Alan's heart; this separation could become permanent and he discovered the quiet love in his heart now set it to beating wildly. Only once had Malcolm had an erection during that voyage and only once had Alan sampled him; it was sufficient to make him feel strongly that he would never again feel such devotion for anyone. He cried out, but his plea was to no avail, for the man was buying only one. The last look Malcolm gave Alan seemed to carry many words. His lips became full, begging for contact; this was lost when his new owner shoved him and Malcolm was forced to climb over the bulwark. Alan felt very alone.

Henry brought only 12 pounds and he set to squealing almost immediately, just as rapidly receiving his first cuff. His descent into the small boat could be traced in yelps and slaps.

"Well?" asked the captain of the lone man who stood with them. "Do you offer 12?" His chances of a good sale were evaporating, and he started at the low figure. The man with the watery blue eyes appeared to be about 50 years of age. His voice, unlike those of the others, was soft and he held an umbrella above his

27

head to shield his pale skin from the burning rays of the sun. His speech was slow.

"The price is high. My means are limited." He looked over Alan again and scratched the short stubble on his chin. "He would not even be able to lift a sack of sugar, he is so narrow in his frame."

"Off with your shirt and let him see how well you are built," the captain ordered as he swung back to the man. "See? The frame is there and will develop within a year, I would venture." He glanced at Alan's prominent ribs and wrinkled his brow. In a pleading tone he asked, "Ten?"

Alan could not classify the man with the umbrella as being bad or good and under this limitation he could not make any finer distinctions. When the man neared and closed his hand on Alan's shoulder, there was a softness to the gesture that was unlike any that had been laid on him in months. There was an easy smile to his face and his eyes seemed kind. If this man did not want him, Alan feared for his life at the hand of the captain.

"My appearance belies it, sir, but I can lift a great weight," he said firmly.

The man's smile spread, and he slipped his hand along the upper arm to feel for biceps. Without being obvious, Alan closed his fist tightly; there was little increase in the girth of his arm. His fingers underwent scrutiny and then the man began on his chest; there was no poking or clawing, just a smooth pass along his ribs and a halt on his breast.

"Ten would be wasted money," the man said as he stepped back. "It would be two years before his strength would come and his keep would be great."

"Nine?" The captain's voice was weak.

"Even at nine, he has most likely caught the pox or the clap from your scurvied crew. Here boy, the breeches, so I can prove you to be marked."

Alan honestly began wondering why people bothered with clothing. His had fared poorly from constant clawing throughout the voyage and he could not help but let a small sigh escape his lips when his breeches settled at his ankles. The captain peered quickly to make sure his goods were whole and, with renewed confidence, announced, "As I thought! There is nothing."

"You could not run a ship so fine—he must then be crawling with the crabs."

The man leaned over and gingerly passed his fingers over the lush crop of black hair that had been growing and spreading around Alan's cock like weeds after a spring rain.

"You will drive me insane!" cried the captain at this point. "Boy! Hoist those breeches. You go for eight pounds—'tis the last I will hear of this."

The man brought himself up to full stature and looked down his nose at the captain. "It's a bad bargain, I am sure," he said. "But it is kinder for me to save this life than to have you take it in the dark of night."

They had not gone too far in the small boat when the man let out a high-pitched laugh, as though a conspiracy were in progress. "If he had but known I would have paid eighteen pounds for you! I took a liking to you the instant I saw you!"

Life with Arnold Steward became as pleasant as life had been at home. Alan did not much care for

Arnold's wife, but neither did she care for her husband and occupied herself with her own interests, retiring to her chamber. Of work there was plenty and Alan spent his first six months in the cane fields with the other slaves and bondsmen. There was no driving overseer and an even pace was maintained. Another birthday passed, and Alan's body began showing promise of what it would become; his shoulders seemed to swell by the day and his biceps became like iron from lifting sacks in the warehouse. The need for deep breath before slinging a sack built capacity in his chest. Alan took to leaving his shirt open so others could admire the physique and the spread of short hair peppering its expanse.

Alan's schedule changed after the day he found sufficient courage to approach the owner in regard to his desire for books. From then on he worked in the field from dawn until the hour before noon, allowing him time for a quick sluicing and a change of clothes. Arnold was not inclined to leave his bed before noon, and it became Alan's duty to carry in his breakfast on a tray. As the man carefully sipped his tea that first morning, he told Alan that he had observed him in the warehouse and wanted to compliment him on his physique. Alan laughed, recalling the way he had been examined on the boat, and imitated his actions by stripping off his singlet. The man nodded his approval. Alan kept looking at Arnold's gentle eyes and their silent request; he responded by releasing his belt and letting his breeches fall.

Arnold set his teacup down with a clatter and his voice seemed tight as he said, "Take this food tray away! We've got to speak of your education." Holding up the tray, he began to kick off the bedcover; the strength exhibited by his rearing cock belied the grey hair about his organs. He passed the tray to Alan and tensely said, "Come into the bed, where we can speak in comfort!"

Arnold's lips formed no words; their moist softness told Alan he could have what he wished as they touched their way through a relentless search of Alan's body. Master and slave lost meaning as Alan turned his position about; he had a fleeting thought of Malcolm as his mouth closed over Arnold's cockhead, but Malcolm had not even tried to do as well. Alan nestled closer and began shifting his chest against Arnold's lightly-haired abdomen when his throat sensed throbbing life. As the hair on his own body was pressed flat by Arnold's smooth chest, Alan's muscles hardened and his actions became vigorous enough to set Arnold's hips jerking. And then there was the sudden expansion in his throat while his own body tensed; his cock began equaling the hot bursts he was receiving.

Alan's time in the fields became minimal, his efforts there usually by his own request for the purpose of working off energy. The major portion of his time was for the enjoyment of comfort, love and Arnold's library. At first there was little to read because most of the books were in Latin or Greek, but Arnold took an interest in the ambitious youth's quest for knowledge and he became an excellent teacher of languages, supplementing his shelves of books by borrowing from other plantation owners. Life held great promise and the years of indenture passed as though Alan were a free man.

After five years of bondage his face radiated intelligence and strong character while ready to burst into a gleaming smile at the slightest stimulus. As far as Arnold was concerned, he had become alarmingly handsome. During their expeditions to Bridgetown, women paused in their walks or leaned over the railings of balconies while men's eyes took on looks of admiration with an undercurrent of desire as they ranged over the magnificent physique.

Alan never seemed to be aware of the looks he received, except to show a constant smile with parted lips. He knew well that he had an attractive appearance and, being on horseback, his seated position in no way concealed the exceptionally narrow hips that exaggerated the broadness of his well-developed shoulders. Against Arnold's wishes, he always let his shirt remain open, leaving no question about the slimness of his waist nor of the shiny pelt which let little of his actual chest be seen. Between his breeches and his shoes, more of his manliness showed in the copious covering on his legs, like thick black wool stockings above the slender bare ankles.

The direct admiration of the people did not distract Alan; he was too devoted to Arnold both by affection and appreciation of the opportunities given. Where Arnold would be alarmed by the reactions in Bridgetown, he found the greatest security in the contentment Alan felt at the plantation and on the beach. Alan would disrobe, break into a run and cleanly cut the water in a surface dive to avoid the black sea urchins with their treacherous spines. After what should have been an exhausting swim, he would race up the sand to fall next to Arnold while laughing joyfully, then turn immediately to his reading, questioning when something was not clear or to gain familiarity with a new word. Arnold was willing to suffer all this while hunched under an umbrella; his reward came each time those eyes lifted from the book and filled with sincere love.

Operating the plantation was primarily handled by the overseer, who wholly reflected Arnold's attitude. It was sufficient to have a plantation and to produce; no one was concerned about profits. Slaves and indentured men led an easy life, never lacking food and never flogged—in fact, the outer leather casing of the one whip on the plantation was covered with cracks from lack of use and absence of the human oils that would impart flexibility. As is the case with most men, such contentment led only to disquiet and heightened the need for action. This action was taken one night in a stormy revolt. If questioned, none would have been capable of supplying a reason for the uprising, but the effect was disaster. Arnold and his wife gave up their earthly interests. Alan, too, almost lost his life because the others thought him to be above their stations, raised there through favoritism. But the bloodlust had already been dissipated when it came to his turn and it required little convincing for him to gain release.

The morning after the revolt gave the men the action they had lacked in their lives. Arnold, it ensued, had gone deeply into debt, to the point where the plantation had not really been his for more than a year. When the slaves and indentured men were rounded up, they learned that their ownership was now in the hands of Benjamin Wilson, the biggest plantation owner on the island. Alan saw his future take a large leap forward under this bondage: The heavy debt and transfer meant that his five years with Arnold were of no value and the term of seven years to work off his indenture was to begin again that day.

Benjamin Wilson, like most of the other planters, placed little stock in the indentured men. The black slave was worth far more, being able to work a full day of hard labor in the cane fields under a relentless sun. Their hours were from a quarter of an hour before sunrise to a quarter of an hour after sunset, with two hours off at midday. Their food was poor. Negligence applied as well to quarters and clothing; those who had been there for more than two months were easily recognized by their blank-eyed looks and by the tattered clothing they wore.

Wilson and his overseer heartily believed that punishment was the most appropriate means of control. Their obsession in this regard showed in their nightly performances and their enjoyment of the suffering they inflicted was openly displayed immediately after the whiplash drew blood instead of raising a welt. If no infraction had been committed and there had been no failures in work, leaving them without a victim, they contrived the slightest excuse to gain one. The setting was dramatic and unreal, having a pillory positioned in an open area at the quarters and illuminated by the light of a bonfire that foiled the hiding darkness of sudden night that set in with the sunset.

To spare further soiling of the tattered clothing and to remove any shielding against the whip, the victim was led or dragged to the platform with his naked body reflecting the flames of the fire in the sweat of fear drenching his flesh. The procedure was always drawn out, thereby increasing the amount of sweat and salinity and make the cuts smart unbearably. As though the whip were not enough, the men feared the pillory where—if a faint overtook them—the lower plank butted against their throats with the threat of strangulation.

Alan was not spared any of this; nightly he had to take his position with the others to observe what they would undergo. His hazard was great, for when he was brought in the overseer's eyes brightened as he looked over the powerful body that could be at his mercy. As a result, work in the warehouse at the plantation house would not be for Alan—the cane fields held his reckoning. There, alongside the slaves, he had to put his body to demanding tasks.

As careful as he tried to be, Alan found himself strongly held and stripped the third night after his arrival. In the light of the bonfire, he was led to the pillory. Different though it would be from tricing and beating on board the ship, a subconscious reaction was connecting the two and dangling was replaced by rigidity. The contempt shown by the overseer and the way he brandished the whip as he loosened the muscles of his arm was something Alan would never forget. The last view he had of the overseer before the top board of the pillory was locked in place made the first bitterness of pure hatred flood his mind.

Chapter Four

Muscled as he was, Alan had to struggle with the gate from the oxcart. Normally, two men would lift it and set it in place. But no one dared approach to assist him; Alan knew why and did not have to look up to confirm the reason. In fact, he *refused* to look up. The overseer's boots were easily recognized and they had appeared within his view the instant he began his struggle. There seemed to be no reason to speed the proclamation that he was due before the pillory that night. Regardless of how it happened, he was the driver when the wheel settled into the rut. The lurch had sprung the gate free. Straining, he bore it aloft and worked it into position. The overseer said nothing until the last of the cane was replaced in the wagon. Alan was about to urge the oxen on.

"Think you've been getting away easy for the past two weeks?" asked the overseer. The sneer made it appear more of a telling than an asking. He snorted. "You may as well know you're being saved for Robert's coming."

"Who's Robert?"

"Wilson's son. Once you meet up with him, you'll think I'm an angel of mercy. Threw him out of Oxford, they did. Said he was too much of a bully on his schoolmates." The twisted smile developed as he looked over Alan's bared torso. "He's always liked them big and muscled. He'll take a good liking to you."

Alan did not know what to make of this information. Could anyone be worse? Was the overseer trying to mislead him? He turned back to the oxen.

"Got each one of your marks down, so you have a good score," the overseer called. "'Twould be no surprise if Robert takes over and cuts you down to size, ugly prick and all!"

Alan nudged the oxen and turned his back to the overseer. He gritted his teeth against the roaring laugh behind him.

Signs of a restive air began showing three days before Robert's ship was due. Alan received only looks of fright when he tried to learn about Robert. The slaves seemed particularly terrified; Alan never knew they could show so much white in their eyes when they opened them wide.

The overseer appeared disgruntled the evening the ship came in. He blasted orders around and had more wood piled on the bonfire until the area was lighted as though it were day. Still, Robert did not show. The overseer's disappointment was obvious when he personally tore the clothing off Alan. He was seething and the acrid smell of his sweated body intensified with his anger. When he pulled off his own singlet to fully free the muscles that would make the whip sound explosive, the slaves began a low, swaying chant and the mournful sound put a chill into Alan's body even though the heat from the flames was scorching.

"What's the matter?" he demanded, grabbing painfully on Alan. "Can't get it up tonight? Got you scared for once?" He jerked the flaccid cock near to uprooting. "You'd better put on a good show if Robert gets here," he threatened, "or you'll never live to know you didn't!"

The slaves who had pinned Alan's arms moved rapidly on the overseer's signal. In low tones they seemed to be mumbling apologies to Alan as they set the pins of the pillory in place. The fright they displayed set Alan's muscles quivering and he fought to still them. He was drawing blood from his tongue with a heavy bite to keep himself from crying out that he did not want to die yet.

Alan knew when that first blow was descending; during all the practice cracks of the whip against the platform, the chant was unvaried. Alan never heard the crack. Every muscle in his body cramped the instant the burning sear ripped over his back. His legs kicked out from under him and he was more willing to take pillory strangulation than the pain flaming over his entire back. Still, he struggled to his feet so he could pull air into his lungs. He would have a few moments before the whip would be raised again, the overseer's way of playing with his victims.

"Damn Robert!" he heard through his pain as the whip flicked back. "He'd enjoy the sight of you. If that crack raised your mule's prick so fast, the next one should unload you, if you don't get to shitting yourself! It's his bad luck to miss this!"

Alan again closed his eyes tightly and held his breath, bracing himself against the pillory. The blow was long in coming. Then Alan heard hooves and the screaming of slaves as they rushed out of the way of the oncoming horses. Alan ventured to open his eyes when the riders halted before the pillory. With the bonfire beyond them, he could make out only silhouetted forms.

"Ho, Robert!" the overseer greeted joyously. "You got here but a moment too late for the first one! You've yet to enjoy more; want to see him pump his life-load like you've never seen before?"

"Hold off a moment; let me have a better look at this one." There was a ring of authority to the voice, but it was not a pleasant one. The rider dismounted and came close to the pillory; he remained a silhouette.

"Now, Robert? But watch for the splash of blood and come else you ruin your good clothes."

There was cunning in the overseer's voice as he said, "Perhaps you'd be wanting to lay it on in your best manner, like you used to before you went to university?"

"No, I think not," said Robert. His hand seemed cold when it touched Alan's bare shoulder before slipping to the haired chest. His fingers curled as they locked on Alan's pelt. Then they were like claws on his stiff cock. "This man is spared! Get two men to take him to my rooms!"

An argument ensued between Robert and his father, the other horseman; Robert was insistent in his need for a personal servant and his father gave in. The overseer spat in disgust.

Alan, through his cloak of pain, marveled at the crispness of the clean linens on which he lay and at the sight of the wholesome food he had no desire to touch. He wondered even more about the deep concern and soft touch Robert had displayed when he carefully bathed Alan's body with a fine-scented soap that could only have come from France.

"That man needs to take a place in the pillory and

have me lay on the lash!" Robert muttered through clenched teeth as he cautiously applied an ointment prepared by the slaves from herbs and oils and concocted in their mysterious fashion.

"This will heal you, have no fear," he continued. "The cut is deep but this substance is one like a miracle." And when the cut was covered, he cleaned his fingers and began stroking Alan's legs and buttocks, the pressure ever increasing. "The man is a fool," he declared. 'I have never seen one so handsome as you, even in England. To think, only a few minutes more and your beautiful flesh would have been like to ribbons."

Robert slipped his hand into the black nest below the cleft and closed it gently about the testicles. Alan sensed a quiver before it was hastily withdrawn. "I must let you sleep. Be careful not to turn over," he advised and was gone.

Thankful for the attention he received in the following weeks, Alan found he could go no further with appreciation. He had no liking for Robert. The short stature, the pudgy body, the puffy skin on the face and the short-fingered hands all combined to assail Alan's sense of attractiveness. The eyes were difficult to look at, appearing to be beady points between puffy lids, and the mouth was like a gash surrounded by the thinnest of lips. But Robert was salvation and Alan tolerated the daily bathing even though capable of attending to it himself. He disliked most of all Robert's close attention to his genitals where, with hands shaking, washing would be most thorough. *Well*, thought Alan, *as long as he keeps his frilly clothes on this form of indenture could be tolerable*.

When Robert was not there, Alan had a great grievance. He was totally alone. The windows were well barred against attack on the household in case of a slave uprising and his door was locked. Fine as the room was, it was still a prison. He longed for some way to gain exercise to stretch the injured muscles into condition, and began pleading for trips to the beach and swimming. He tried to counter Robert's fear for the healing cut with the thought that salt water would be most beneficial. Robert did not give in until the wound was completely closed and even then he required escort by another indentured man, while he himself carried a whip and a pistol.

Alan sensed a form of impatience on Robert's part during their time at the beach and, after a good swim, his suggestion to return was met with reluctance. Then, when they finally did leave, Robert would drive the horse hard until their mouths were crested with foam.

"Now," said Robert, his eyes looking feverish, his back up against the locked door and with pistol pointed at both of them, "you'll both divest and be quick about it!"

Alan's blood boiled when the other man—he was called John—smiled and began pulling off his singlet. It would have been so simple for them to have rushed Robert, but he was complying and looking pleased. Perhaps they could have escaped with greater ease from the house than from the quarters and could have stowed away on a vessel bound for Jamaica, which had been taken by the English only a few years before. Perhaps it would have been their fates to have been captured, branded on their forehead with FT—for "Fugitive Traitor"—and been flogged. Perhaps…

"Alan! Be quick!"

41

It was better to follow the example, else the iron bar he had hidden beneath his belt and body at the beach might have been found. He was most careful to keep it covered as he released his breeches and stepped out of them.

"The bed, Alan. Get on the bed!" Robert was handling the pistol easily, but his tenseness was threat of easy triggering.

Alan's muscles tightened when he neared the bed. Resignation swept through him when he saw the manacles and chains which had been attached while they were at the beach. If Robert had been able to read what this submission meant, he would have known that Alan was only playing for time and had set his mind on escape to Jamaica.

But Robert saw something different. "Oh, Alan my love," he exclaimed, "you do want me! Yes, put your arms back and let John fasten them."

Robert looked weak in the knees as he eased himself into a chair where he could command a full view. His pistol and whip remained firmly held, but he kept the butt of the weapon buried in his crotch, rubbing. He gave a great sigh.

"You are beautiful! The sea has given great richness to your hair. How thick it is in the pits of your arms! Your body, so long and beautiful and so hidden in soft blackness.

"Hurry, John—that's it, his ankles! Oh, Alan, you will show your love for me. John's lips can make any man soar and I do want you to show you can make it as hard and great as it was when first I saw you. How I've longed to see you that way when I bathed you!" His eyes became distant. "But I had to heal you…"

The sound of Robert's voice was almost sickening to Alan. It was witless of him to have permitted manacling. Robert was mad and there was no telling what he would do now that Alan was powerless. John looked almost as bad; when Robert had complimented him, John's groin had stirred into life. Now, as he turned away from the manacles at Alan's ankles, he proudly drew back the skin and exposed the hardness of his pointed cockhead.

At least it was clean, Alan thought. "Now John, now!" Robert cried and let his mouth hang open as his eyes brightened. He dropped his pistol and began squirming in the chair as John buried his face in Alan's crotch. Robert's freed hand was clutching at his own uneasy groin.

Alan knew that under other circumstances, the darting tongue and warm mouth would have had him already past the point of bursting, but now he remained flaccid. A strange pity was developing for Robert, for *anyone* who had to get this thrills this way. Alan looked at Robert and showed his helplessness to accommodate.

Robert caught this look and leapt out of his chair with amazing agility, laying the whip across John's back in the same movement. Even before John's muscles smoothed in ration and his sucking took on greater vigor, Robert was crying out, "Alan! For my love, you must! You must!"

Deep inside John's throat, muscles echoed the spasm of his body as the whip struck again. The tightness, the warmth and, above all, a will to keep John from being beaten for his fault started to fill Alan's cock with solidity. For all his expertise, John had to back off from the new size—and yet, he managed to intensify his attack.

Alan no longer had to concentrate; his abdomen hollowed deeply in his fight to delay the hastening action of the vibrating tongue and sliding lips. The chains from his wrists snapped loudly when he yanked to their limit as his first burst blasted into John's mouth. His body began twisting violently as John maintained his same frenzy, forcing for all the bursts Alan could possibly achieve. Alan suddenly stilled, only the shaking of his chest showing how wracked his body had been; he turned his head weakly.

Robert seemed nearly exhausted, his face heavily flushed: "Now, John, now! I must see!" he was saying anxiously, his puffy lids lifted, which made his eyes look beadier than ever.

John let Alan's cock slip free; it hovered low over the abdomen. Slowly he released all his mouth held, letting it coat the length of the cock to the dripping hair on the belly. The last of it was released onto Alan's testicles, well mixed with sputum. From his crouched position, John rose to his knees and looked at Robert imploringly. He was greatly excited; the loose skin was now held back on the bony-looking shaft by the greatly distended cockhead.

In a way, John had great possibilities, Alan decided. The fair body with bare chest and stiff cock rearing out of auburn hair deserved attention, but not while he was in chains.

"Will you bring me on, Master Wilson?" John was pleading. His fluids had already wet the darkened tip held at the severe angle, and more flowed with each rocking throb. "Please, Master Wilson?"

Robert was staring with wonder at Alan's soaked genitals. Without taking his eyes off them, he nodded his head slowly and said, "You did not swallow one drop, John, but saved it all for me. There is so much! Yes, I shall gladly bring you on: Double it, John! You can, you know."

John fell forward, suspending himself on stiff arms and feet directly above Alan. Although agony shattered his features each time the whip fell on him, the times between showed a strange ecstasy. His cock paralleled his abdomen and when his forces broke free, most was buried deeply in the hair on Alan's chest.

"Out, out John! Quick!" Robert raced to unlock the door.

The heavy breathing and look on Robert's face gave John no pause or delay. He scooped up his clothing and raced into the hall, cock still pounding, still vertical up against his body. Alan dreaded what was to come next: It was bad enough to have been wet in that manner by his own fluid and then John's, but Robert's would be sickening. Like the rest of his body, Robert's parts—barely emerging from their surrounding hair—were disgusting.

Alan least expected the sudden transition: Robert once again became the tenderest of creatures and was almost in tears, profuse in his apologies for having laid on the whip, as though it were Alan who had felt the lash. Again, Alan began to feel faintly sorry for him, and suffered through the slobbering on his neck and face.

"My dearest dear," Robert was mumbling, "if I had known you would give so much love for me I would not have used the whip to hasten you. Please, oh please, forgive me?"

"I do forgive you," said Alan, hoping desperately that this would bring his release from the manacles. His arms were aching.

But Robert kept mumbling on. "Oh, my love, I do not deserve one as good or as kind as you," he was saying as his kisses gained ardor in keeping with his declaration. Subtly they changed into sucking, bringing marks to Alan's neck and shoulders. He suddenly stopped and buried his fingers in Alan's pelt, where the hair was still dry.

"It is thoughtless of me," he said. "Here I am feasting on you while your essence cools!"

Alan's stomach churned as Robert's tongue began swabbing at his testicles; his cock seemed to shrivel under cleaning. Alan's mouth acquired a sour taste when the hard-working tongue began darting into the heavy hair and fervid moans marked the discovery of thick accumulations. Futilely he again tested the manacles, wishing his hands were free to shield his ears from the sounds this madman was making. Forcing abidance, Alan waited for the moment when it would all be over. When it was near, Robert's body convulsed erratically and then the tongue was swiftly returned to pick up new wetness from Alan's furry thighs. The moans rose to an ecstatic pitch.

Chapter Five

Much to Alan's relief, only John returned daily to serve his meals and attend to chamber duties. In body and face, John became more appealing with each day. Alan found John likeable in an odd way—he appreciated the kind attitude and the personal interest but did not fully understand the man's masochistic streak, even though he himself had been brought to orgasm by a belt or a whip.

"No, 'tis not strange," John was explaining one day. "Master Wilson's needs are not as great as mine or, I would guess, yours," he said with a meaningful glance. "I have seen others like you give such great satisfaction that Master Wilson did not return for as much as a month."

"'Twould be a relief," Alan admitted, trying to estimate whether he could manage his escape in that time. The iron bar he had smuggled into the room was doing its work, but at a painfully slow rate. The bars had been set deep into holes in the stone walls around the windows and as he dared not hammer, it became a matter of wearing away the stone scrape after scrape. He glanced up at John, suddenly realizing the import of his words. "When you say you've seen others… then I am not the first for this?"

"I've served Master Wilson for four years, since he was 15."

"As a manservant?"

John formed a wry smile. "As a sex servant would be a better way of saying it. Each came from the pillory; I was the first he had seen throw my spunk under the lash."

"'Tis a great pity if it needs the lash to bring it forth—I could not accommodate you that way. 'Tis greater pity to have to wait a week or a month." A slight tingle raced from his groin as he recalled John's adept tongue. "I am already near overflowing," Alan confessed, "though it has been only two days."

John spun around from the task of making the bed. His eyes were bright as he said, "Master Wilson has already left. There is a party of sorts at one of the plantations and he will be gone all the day. It would please me to serve you."

Alan frowned: "But I could not whip you."

"'Twould not be necessary, if you would tolerate my spunk in your hair. I have only seen slaves as magnificent as you—the sight of it sets my spunk to boiling."

Alan glanced down at the ring of moisture spreading where his breeches peaked highest. Slowly he began undoing his belt.

John was true to his word: He raised Alan to a fevered climax and caught the contagion. He had barely spit Alan's load on the hairy abdomen before he sank his cock into it and began slamming his lower reaches against Alan's belly. To John's most sensitive part the heavy fur was as grinding as grit and equal in punishment to the whip; Alan soon felt the tense vibrations mounting in his body. He did not know what prompted him, but he cupped his hands over John's nipples and suddenly gripped tightly. John gave a sharp cry that was fully a groan and collapsed on Alan; his cries became sharper with each burst. He seemed beyond himself, for Alan's brutal massage continued.

With each passing day, each scrape of the bar against the stone at the window brought greater conviction to Alan's mind that he should bring John into his plans for escape. Where Alan had ventured into the fringes of sadism without causing any grievous hurt, their daily searches for relief in each other's bodies had proved John very capable of matching Alan's stride. He knew John would be willing to join him, not because he sought freedom that greatly but because he feared losing Alan, all the while in full accord because Alan's life near Robert was misery.

Alan decided that John would be included at the last minute, when the grill could be spring free. He worked diligently, encouraged by the need to bring freedom to someone other than himself. In his fumbling, Alan almost lost his digging tool out the window. It was afternoon, a full three weeks since Robert's last visit and the sound of the key being inserted in the lock was not like that of the head servant. Alan was barely able to put the tool from sight and take a stance at the window, as though some bit of flora in the freedom of the garden had suddenly merited interest. He turned slowly to take in Robert's posture at the open door, the legs stiff and widespread, full of authority, the pistol in one hand and the dragging whip in the other. Alan smiled at Robert and began pulling off his singlet, wondering if John could meet the challenge after their exorbitance that morning.

"Robert," he addressed him in a calm voices, as he stepped free of his breeches, "'tis love we have for you if you cast aside the whip and leave my hands free."

"No!" Robert cried out. "You will cheat me! John needs the whip, else he throws little for me. See, see how he needs it!"

Practice had leant perfection to the flick of his wrist, which carried the whip from the floor with a resounding crack. Robert sounded enraptured as he said, "Watch his spunk fill his prick to stiffness!"

John recoiled from the strike with a scream and flung his hands up to cover his face, then sank to the floor moaning with pain. Blood was beginning to trickle between his fingers and over the back of one hand. Alan felt a wash of hatred rise and lunged at Robert, who dropped the whip and slipped into the hall, screaming with terror and pulling the door closed behind him. His impetus made Alan slam against the door and he pounded furiously even after Robert's screaming had faded. Frustrated, he turned and set his back against the door. John was still crouched on the floor and blood had already trickled down his arm. His moans were pitiful.

Alan had barely begun staunching the flow from the cut—which appeared dangerously close to John's left eye—when the door was thrown open with enough force to send it crashing against the wall. Three slaves accompanied Robert, all swarthy men. Two made straight for Alan and caught his arms, lifting to his feet as though he had the lightness of an empty sack. The third took hold of John and dragged him up.

"At the pillory," Robert cried out, once more full

of authority. The hand holding the pistol denied that; it was white and shaking badly. His beady eyes were fixed on Alan as he said, "You need a lesson, and a good one I shall provide!"

Robert did not have the strength of the overseer, but his handling of the whip managed to lay open John's flesh, cut after cut. Alan saw him take advantage of a body bent by the pillory; the whip strokes doubled the torture, being laid not only on the back but, with the backhand flip, being laid on the chest and abdomen. Robert seemed tireless, unsatisfied with the flaps of skin hanging from the chest and the pools of blood on the platform. He had John revived with a pail of water before he brought out the most excruciating cry, one completely inhuman, as the tip of the whip cut through the testicles. Alan fought the bonds that firmly anchored his wrists to a hitching post when John's unrecognizable body crumpled.

Alan experienced neither fear of the whip nor of the guarding slaves, only the need to wrap his fingers around Robert's throat before he would undergo the same torture. The bonds were solid and he witnessed Robert's final act: Jamming the butt of the whip into John's crotch. Alan set his mouth firmly when Robert walked toward him.

"This is for your doing," Robert told him, before continuing to the house. He was breathing heavily and dragged the whip behind him, letting the dirt clean it of John's blood, letting drops fall from the butt.

Back in his room, Alan threw himself on the bed and wept bitter tears, cursing his birth, cursing the will that had made him leave home and cursing most strongly the madman who owned him. When he got back to digging at the stone around the window bars, each stroke began lifting flecks instead of just scraping. His determination to escape fed the forces in his hands and the hammer was not needed to drive the tool into the stone. As his hands hardened and perceptible progress could be seen for each hour's work, Alan began to modify his plan. Between the time of his escape and from the room and his escape from the plantation, he would drive his digging tool deep into Robert's temple.

The deeper he dug, the softer the stone seemed to be. He could see the end of his task coming near, with only another half inch to clear. He applied himself with greater concentration, making each dig pay. Absorbed as he was, he started with utmost fright when the thick black arm came over his shoulder and reached for the tool in his hand. He looked up quickly and saw that the owner was one of the most powerful of the slaves. Beyond him, Robert was in his typical posture at the door, whip and pistol ready.

"I was very hurt, Alan," he was saying slowly, "when I caught sight of what you were doing. 'Tis over a week since John left us and I have neglected you. If you wanted to get out and look for me, why did you not think of calling for me? I would have come immediately. Also, I cannot go about searching if you are not here when I have come for your love. You must always be ready for me."

"Your love is *shit*!" Alan spat at him, his eyes glaring.

"Take him to the bed, Trysk. I want him kept safe."

Alan sprang up, but the overpowering bulk of the

slave held command. The powerful arms wrapped around him and carted him to the bed, where he was dropped like a toy. Robert's next order had the slave stretching Alan's arms upward, but when it came to applying the manacles, Alan got one arm free. Between the arm and his unsecured legs, he managed to get in some healthy blows; but they did not seem to faze the man. With one arm manacled, the slave turned his attention to the legs, stopping their thrashing by sitting on Alan's knees. Alan cursed until both wrists and ankles were caught. His chest heaving, he waited for Robert's next move—it came too quickly.

"Trysk, his clothes! Take them off him!"

"But Master Wilson—for that I got to free him again."

Robert looked baffled by his oversight, but only for a moment. "Rip them off!" he ordered. "He will not need them any longer."

The slave's strength made the coarse fabric seem like fine paper. But his fingers were nimble as they released and removed Alan's belt at the end. He stood back and surveyed Alan's body.

"Trysk, ever see a white man with so much?"

Trysk shook his head—"Not with most men of any kind, Master Wilson."

Alan tugged at the chains until the manacles began cutting into his wrists when Robert said, "You should see his greatness when he has my love. I want you to see it… yes, you must let him see yours as well. Trysk, your clothes, so he can see how well built you are!"

Trysk's forehead was beaded with perspiration and he glanced at the menacing pistol in Robert's hand. Slowly he began following the orders, his skin glistening with sweat by the time he stood fully naked.

"Trysk, you were not so limp when you were with Jacumbo. I have watched you take him and now I want to see your black flesh against Alan's white."

Alan lay silent with amazement as he watched the heavy stem began to lift the purplish-red tip in pulsating shifts; when the dark veins began showing Alan could see clearly that the proportions were far greater than his own. Alan fought his chains frantically, crying out loudly that he could not cope with such size as Robert said, "With spit, Trysk, as with Jacumbo."

As Trysk finally mounted, his voice was filled with compassion; "I'll try to make it easy on you, but it will hurt—you a handsome man and the sight makes me right hard."

Alan felt the increasing pressure and the pain was murderous, even though Trysk paused when Alan was able to contract behind the flaring head, which seemed the size of a fist. Alan never knew what pain could be like until Robert's whip cracked on Trysk's buttocks. He knew he had fainted because when awareness set in, Trysk's arms were beneath him, powerfully crushing his chest while it seemed his vitals were being rearranged with each plunging stroke that was hastened by the whip. He felt too weak to cry out as the muscled body pressed harder than ever against his haunches and he felt the filling from each heavy throb. Darkness overtook him again.

The soft moaning sounds, Alan realized, came from his own throat. There was no longer the heavy weight of another body on him and his skin felt cold from evaporating perspiration. He seemed to lack any feeling in his hindquarters and weakly forced his head about to see over his shoulder. Trysk was gone. There was only the naked Robert crouching with his face buried, tongue desperately seeking the man's sperm. A dry retching intensified Alan's agony.

Alan did not dare look again when Robert landed his fist solidly in the small of Alan's back, exclaiming, "*Faugh*—you bleed!"

The ever-rising pitches and intensity of voices lifted Alan sufficiently from his stupor to learn he was the central figure in an argument. Benjamin Wilson was nearly explosive in his comments and Robert was crying out his defenses. Alan turned his head slowly and blinked his eyes to bring them into focus. Benjamin's attention was fixed on Alan with a look of disgust and he was paying no to attention to Robert, still as naked as when he had been caught and wildly gesticulating. Behind them, Trysk was motionless with eyes wide. It was Trysk who had reported Robert to his father and Robert was now demanding his life.

Benjamin's voice carried over Roberts' by virtue of its calm strength as he ordered, "Trysk, go—get him to the infirmary. See if anything can be done."

Chapter Six

"You all right, sir?"

It was Trysk's face that Alan managed to separate from the shadows.

"You got to drink this. From Mama Luke, in the kitchen. This is the sixth time for trying."

Alan offered no resistance and began swallowing small sips of a steaming, bitter brew. Its taste repulsed him and he tried to turn away.

"Mama Luke have many teas. She have good magic—you got to drink this."

Trysk's voice warranted confidence and Alan managed to drain the mug. When his head was put down on the straw where he lay, it swam with giddiness and any thoughts he formed melted into haziness. The heavy smell of raw garlic and herbs seemed of no consequence when Trysk opened the tiny earthen jar. Alan wanted only to go back to sleep.

"I must turn you over, gentle like. Mama Luke say you need this, morning and night. I be gentle with you, but I got to stick the finger far."

His voice continued in a soft way, carrying both expressions of the guilt he felt and his fear of Robert. Alan heard little of it, the voice having lulled him to sleep.

Alan's will to live was revived by Trysk and Mama Luke, who chanced wrath by visiting as frequently as possible. In a subtle fashion, Mama Luke brought all her powers into play and changed her concoctions in keeping with his progress. It was she who told Alan that Benjamin had laid down the law to Robert, that he was to stop playing and become a man. Benjamin was pressuring marriage to the daughter of another plantation owner. Mama Luke was irate about this: In her opinion, the girl was the most beautiful on the island and was fine in every regard—voice, manner and education. She threatened that if the marriage were announced she would see to it that her powers revoked all of Robert's sexual interests. She frightened Trysk, for as her temper waxed she turned on him and threatened the same.

Mama Luke also became Alan's defender. She stood up to the overseer and Benjamin both the day the overseer requested control over Alan, boldly insisting that straining would only have Alan bleed to death before the overseer had the opportunity to flog him to death. She, too, carried a deep hatred for them, but reconciled complaisance with the fact that she had no place better to go were she given the opportunity. Alan, his thoughts again turning to escape, tried to entice Trysk and Mama Luke, suggesting that if it were against her will to poison the household food outright, it was within her power to slip at least six of them some powerful sleeping potion. He received outright refusal.

The more Alan thought about escape, the more convinced he became that accomplices were essential. There was little hope for any of the men in the infirmary, since the majority were highly weakened by fevers, which abounded in the islands. Mama Luke had been explicit in her cautions to Alan about avoiding these men. She fretted about the temperatures Alan had been running, yet seemed certain that the fever he displayed was only due to his body's natural reaction to its injuries. Contact and proximity were almost unavoidable, for the infirmary was a crude structure with barred windows and a door that was pegged on the outside. There was no furniture in the room and only piles of straw to serve in place of pallets. If a man was ill enough to be in the infirmary, it was expected that he had need of nothing other than a place to lie.

The inevitable became obvious when Alan awakened one night with his body shaking from chills and his temperature soaring. Dripping with perspiration, his throat and lips were parched. Mama Luke made a brief check the next morning and returned with a steaming mug; the bitter liquid contained extracts from barks, she had explained as she forced him to down it. The brew seemed to help, but his fever still raged. Alan's thinking was far from clear, constantly clouded with deliriums which were hidden holes of horror.

Weeks passed before Alan became capable of forcing his mind to carry simple chains of thought. His mind began to dwell on the condition of his body and he began giving up all hopes, handing himself over to doom. Even in his youthful years, at a time when the rate of growth was highest, his wrists had never appeared so thin nor had his ribs been so prominent. His hipbones seemed to ride inches above his sunken abdomen.

The entire group from the infirmary looked like walking skeletons in the torchlight when they were rudely taken from their piles of straw and herded into the wagon outside the door. It was a moonless night and darkness wrapped around the wagon the instant it was driven beyond the circle of light. The ride was rough, but no one particularly cared. Each was engrossed in the shaking from chills or the burning of fever. What seemed worse was the struggle over the sands of a beach that fronted a cove.

When they neared the water, the glow from the tropical night was sufficient to show a ship. Several men were on the sand and as the wagon approached one emitted a coded whistle. The plantation owner responded and urged the cadavers onto the beach; will-less creatures that they were, each hastened his steps on command… but this was only in his mind and they stumbled slowly.

The ship which brought them to Hispaniola belonged to a Spanish trader who amassed his fortune from legitimate transport of products between the Spanish islands and, under furtive cover of darkness obtained worthless slaves and indentured men for practically nothing from English or French plantation owners with no conscience regarding the value of human life. His sale of these men brought little more than his outlay into his pocket, but each extra coin added to his wealth. At Santa Jago, he managed to dispose of Alan and one other of the men.

The fevers and illnesses of the Englishmen were a matter of contempt to the Spaniards. They pressed the emaciated bodies to work relentlessly in blazing sun and overseers had developed the finest mastery of their whips. While the workers were nearly threadbare, the Spaniards looked regal in the black and severe clothing

Philip II prescribed during his reign. Since the heretical Englishmen were destined to burn in Hell, the relentless sun and minimal clothing served to prepare them for what they would suffer through eternity. The Spaniard, by contrast, was to have only hands and head exposed. The body was thoroughly covered to force the highest degree of morality and, coincidentally, to lessen assault on the olfactory senses of others. Maintenance of this surface aspect bore no relationship to their carnality. Men were men and women were women and their scents were part of their animalistic copulation. The number of members in each plantation family attested to this fact; the way they had to protect their virginal daughters was further proof.

Nevertheless, the Spaniard felt he had a right to display his arrogance. Their devotion to God and the converts they gathered—or the heretics burned at the stake through the Inquisition—were sufficient to keep them in His sight above all others. The fact that they broke out with blasphemous cursing against the slightest thing was offset by the number of times they crossed themselves each day seeking blessing.

The strange, subconscious will for life man can acquire under the most adverse conditions carried Alan's body through the years. The hard-packed earth in the slave quarters wiped out dreams of beds and linens, and he accepted it as a place he could lie. Food was what he ate, never considering that even hogs would push their snouts past it in search of nourishment. When he curled up close to a man at night there was no sexual need in the action; it was a necessity to keep some warmth in his body. His breeches had ripped up the sides a long time before and his shirt was like a draped rag; neither covered enough at night. He found no difference from one day to the next. Like the other men, he discovered satisfaction in the free moments when he could scratch his chest or abdomen or groin, where vermin and follicular infections concentrated. He could take vicious revenge on the vermin when he picked them out, but the infection was another matter. Being so hirsute, there was little of his body where the nerve ends in each hair were not signaling attack.

In time, his mind came to accept the onrush of fever and the itching as normal to his existence. Emaciated beyond recognition, there were only his eyes to indicate continued functioning of his brain. His facility with languages, proven under Arnold's tutelage, enabled him to develop and understanding of the Spanish language in so far as it was used by the overseer. It was a limited vocabulary, but enough to acquire a good accent. His powers of concentration returned slowly but, once functioning, his mind began roving. Among the matters it considered was the ever-pressing need to escape.

Through the preceding 15 months, Santa Jago and Hispaniola were only names for where he was. The plantation was outside the city walls, but not close enough to the jungle. Careful questioning brought him the knowledge that the seacoast was about 30 miles to the south. He began recalling the rough maps Arnold had and the fact that Tortuga was off the northern shore at a distance which could be navigated by canoe. The small island was under Spanish control, but was also the center for the French *filibustiers*. His best course of action was to gain the jungle and make his way to the north shore. He ignored the alarm sounding out the impossibility of travel through the jungle—if life as he was living it was possible, so was the jungle. It was imperative that he get to Tortuga. In some way he would then be able to get passage to English-held Jamaica, even if he had to join the *filibustiers*.

Chapter Seven

Alan was unable to develop a satisfactory plan for escape. Most of the men did not have the will to join him and those who still dreamed of freedom labeled his thoughts of crossing the jungle foolhardy. That is, until Michael Landon was thrown into the compound like a spitting, snarling animal. He was from a buccaneering vessel out of Jamaica that had attacked a Spanish ship south of Hispaniola. They underestimated the crew's power and the Spaniards finished them off rapidly. He was one of the few pulled out of the water and sold in Santa Jago. Alan's eyes took on new life as he observed the man's effrontery and defiance of muskets and pistols to hurl one insult after another at his new owners. The frail frame that was Alan's came up straight and stood tall as Landon approached the hut.

"The bloody bastards," Landon was shouting vehemently. "Oh, for a good bloody pike in my hands. I'd ram the bloody thing up their bloody bums! Give me a cutlass—oh, for my hands with a bloody cutlass! I'd flip their bloody bollocks off so fast they'd fly straight into their bloody mouths and bloody well choke them to death." He halted suddenly at the doorway. "Oh, good Lord above, what a bloody filthy pigsty!" he bellowed at the backs of the departing owners. "You bloody bastards!" The fist he was shaking was clenched so tightly that it was startlingly white above the sun-bronzed arm.

"Calm yourself, man."

Landon swung back and squinted to see into the darkness.

"Who's the bloody Englishman?" he demanded, looking at all the faces in a fast sweep.

"I am," said Alan, "and so are most of the others. Aren't you?"

"You're bloody right I am, and proud of it too! I be Michael Landon."

His periods of calm lengthened as he learned more about what had made these men as they were. His voice became very quiet, but showed his resolve. "Within a week, I'll be out of here!" That was when Alan decided to disclose his thoughts for escape.

Michael had a great many reservations, but the greatest enthusiasm. He began to evolve a plan that started with killing the overseer when he came to lock the huts and compound for the night. His corpse inside and all appearing to be in order without could delay suspicion of escape, giving the men sufficient time to reach the edge of the jungle. Alan's familiarity with the plantation and the habits of the Spaniards helped spur the plan along. Each piece of information—the lay of the cane fields, the locations of trees and drainage ditches—was taken anxiously by Michael. The fact that Alan was contributing toward their goal and feeling useful again began renewing his spirit. Frail as he appeared to be, the look in his eyes showed a newfound strength had been discovered within.

Another spark also caught to rekindle life in

Alan: Midday siestas became a time for plotting rather than sleeping. While the other men were resting their weary bodies, Alan and Michael spent the time at a corner of the hut where a rough table and benches were used at meal times. With a stick, Michael made marks on the earth floor to outline Hispaniola and Tortuga. He would sit upright for the longest time in silence, staring at the map with great concentration and, when a detail would be recalled from memory he would look at Alan as though truly inspired, hitch his breeches above his knees and double over to put down new marks. Minor as the detail might be, Alan invariably caught the enthusiasm and was apt to drop to the floor on hands and knees or squat next to Michael's far-flung leg in anticipation of a revelation.

One of them turned out to be a startling discovery: Michael had paused just as he was about to make one of his marks and, in his doubled up position, turned his face to Alan as though in doubt. Fearful of interrupting a thought, Alan remained silent, but his eyes were fixed on Michael's as though he was trying to will resolution into the other man's mind.

"I wish those bloody Spaniards would give us razors or something to take your bloody beard off!"

Not expecting this in the midst of plotting, Alan frowned to orient himself. "Why?" he asked. Recovering, he continued, "You should see your own bloody face, as you would say it. Besides, it hides the drawn look I have."

Michael studied him for a long moment, then he said softly, "Your lips in that bloody forest put a strain on my vitals and your bloody hand has my bloody blood boiling!"

Alan's face flushed red as he discovered he had been skimming Michael's calf, lightly ruffling the surface covering of hair that he saw shimmering in the sunlight like a veil of gold. He let his hand remain so occupied and looked back at the face with the large eyes as blue as the tropical sky and the long blond hair swept back in deep waves by the binding thong. Michael was bringing his face closer and Alan's parted lips began reaching. The compound and Santa Jago disappeared; the forest grew quickly over the plantations and the exotic birds multiplied, their calls blending into the sweetest of music and Michael's hand swept over Alan's cock like a gentle surf.

"Oh, Lord above!" cried Michael. "What bloody kind of a bloody hitching post do you carry in your bloody breeches!"

Alan was unaware of the earth floor against his bony knees; he only knew that his mouth was at last upon that well-defined chest. He was also aware that his ragged shirt was being slipped off his sharp shoulders. Michael, in the manner of buccaneers, had been in action with bare chest and legs and had nothing more to wear at the plantation than his breeches. The fine gold hair of his chest shimmered as brightly as the veil on his legs. As Alan released the belt around Michael's waist and spread the breeches, darker hair came into sight and Alan continued on his course. He had not known how great was his hunger until Michael's fingers began gripping his shoulders tightly. Alan drew hard along Michael's length to let his thirst be known and with the emotion of his awakening shook fiercely as the fire inside him was quelled by surge after surge.

Michael at last inched Alan away, having to be forceful about it. With a hand on each side of the heavily bearded face, he looked long and hard into the dark eyes. His lips were like heated irons when they crushed Alan's.

"You bloody bastard!" he said afterward. "You couldn't wait and cheated me!"

He was not being as critical as he sounded.

"Skin and bones are not enough for a man," said Alan, fully conscious of how his body looked. His touch at Michael's chest expressed his admiration for the feel of muscled flesh.

"'Tis not the appearance of a man, Alan, but what is within that holds merit. I warrant you lack good meat, except on that bloody hitching post, but I find you exceedingly handsome." As if catching himself embarrassed by this display of softness, he added emphatically, "Bloody well handsome!" Boldly, with exaggeration, he took to examining Alan's body. "And if I had a bloody black cover like yours," he continued, "I'd go about stark naked to show it for all its beauty!"

Alan surveyed the blackness on his front; along a broad midline, across his chest and at the abdomen, no skin showed through. Probing fingers rarely brought his nipples to light. He glanced at the ragged cloth of the floor; slowly he reached for the singlet and rolled it into a ball. Alan broke into a smile such as he had not shown in nearly two years when he threw the shirt against the wall. He would no longer need it—he would be enveloped with warmth enough through the night, Michael's warmth.

Preparations for Easter of 1659 seemed to carry through from the days before the Lenten period at the plantations. The slaves and indentured men were always most thankful for religious holidays, which gave them respite from floggings and excessive labor. The Spaniards found it a necessity to consecrate their souls at this holy season, though the week after Easter these same men became the most unholy of creatures and the whip was laid on heavily. Michael, after consulting about their practices of the previous year, decided that Holy Wednesday—between Palm Sunday and Easter—would be the most propitious time for their escape. From then, every moment was dedicated to preparation and detailed review of their plan.

With Alan's help, Michael collected items they could steal, most having no apparent value but which he deemed essential. Among these was a strip of thin leather: Between them they chewed the leather into pliable softness and pounded it between stones at siesta time to make it thinner and longer. With a bit of broken stone, they managed to cut it into thongs and a pouch, which Michael fashioned into a sling. Once it proved operationally successful, he seemed relieved to know that at least they had a defensive weapon, one they could also use in the jungle to kill birds for food.

Nearly all their planning and preparation appeared to be wrecked the day before they were to test their fate. The plantation had broken into rampant activity and all the workers were recalled from the fields. Most were locked in the compound, but Alan, Michael and a few others were put to work carting valuables out of the house or at digging holes in which these were to be buried. Even the well acquired a large quantity of items. The amount of silver and gold the house contained was beyond belief: From the outside it was relatively modest in appearance, but within was a storehouse of wealth. The Spaniards' anxiety for these precious items and the need to hide them was great: A Spanish captive had escaped and arrived at the fort in Santa Jago that morning to tell them that Morgan, the buccaneer, had anchored his vessels at Puerta de Plata and at this very moment was marching his men for attack.

According to Michael, the Spaniards did well to fear Morgan, who had proved himself highly capable with Robert Venables when the English took Jamaica. Recently he had joined Captain Jackman, John Morris and William Dampier, whose raids and attacks had become the talk of Jamaica. Morgan's threats and actions were all calculated to instill fright in the hearts of the men from whom he demanded ransom. His favorite threat had become one in which he stated coldly that if the ransom were not forthcoming, then men would see their wives and children torn to pieces before they would be disemboweled, one by one.

The plantation's fear of Morgan began transferring to Alan by late afternoon, when he was pressed into service to help harness teams of horses to the two carriages that would whisk the family away to the safety of the Fort in Santa Jago. The horses sensed the fear around them as well, and they quivered, snorted and pawed with impatience. In his haste to get the carriages to the house, the overseer cursed Alan badly for being in the way and causing the horses to rear. As the overseer finally cracked his whip over their heads to race them to the house, the owner's son did likewise to his team; their carriages rocked wildly as the harnesses pulled tight. Michael moved swiftly:

The sling whistled above his head and the second team of horses reared high when the stone bit into a flank. The horses broke into a gallop, their ears flat on their heads, eyes wide and mouths open in terror. They veered at the back of the first carriage, but only enough to clear themselves. Carriage wheels added their own din as they ground together just before the first wagon began tilting. In a cloud of dust, the overseer and the owner's son lost their fear of Morgan while meeting death.

The wails now coming from the house were pitiable. To frustrate attackers and prevent the escape of slaves, all other horses had been scattered in the fields. Their only means of conveyance now showed as a trail of dust raised by hooves, reins and broken traces. Michael urged Alan to follow his lead and they arrived at their hut not a moment too soon, for the owner and two of his sons appeared with pistols. They had had enough trouble and were desperate to avoid more by locking in their slaves. Even with a pistol in his hand, the younger son made it clear that he was frightened at the thought of being on the plantation instead of in the security of the fort. His father was terse in saying that they would all be well hidden and Morgan would never find them.

Chapter Eight

The side foray of Morgan's men arrived at the plantation while the cannonade was reaching a peak. Although slaves and indentured men had little to fear from the buccaneers, apprehension was evident while they huddled at the far end of the hut, the farthest they could get from the wild cries and gruff voices of the men breaking in the door. Only Michael cheered.

When freedom became theirs, Alan found a handful of buccaneers had already routed the family from their hiding places. Two of the crew had been unable to restrain themselves and were graphically demonstrating what would happen to the other daughters and wife, with one holding down a girl's arms while the other was vigorous in his rape. One of the sons lay in a pool of blood, his head split down to his breastbone and the mother was on the ground in a dead faint.

The yells from the digging men, led by Alan and Michael, were echoed by loud screams from the father and then from the older boy. As he helped pile the valuables in the open, Alan's concave abdomen drew in even farther when he saw the father pulling himself painfully along the ground, his entrails dragging in the dust, toward the daughters who were being implanted lustfully. The son was only staring wild-eyed at his hands, overflowing with hot bowels. Alan grabbed a cutlass and, though far from doing a neat job, put the boy out of his misery. He was about to do the same for the father, but remembered the man's lack of compassion in applying a whip to bare backs.

During the trek from Santa Jago to Puerta de Plata, Alan discovered Michael was distributing his load of valuables between two of the grumbling men who were staggering with their loads. Although Alan had been given little to carry, he could not understand Michael's rapid unburdening until he was swept up into the arms he had come to know so well. He was in the midst of his demands to be put down when he realized what Michael had foreseen: The fever brought on by the excitement. That was the last he knew about their progress to the ships.

Only one period of clarity came to Alan during their voyage: He had opened his eyes slowly and a weak smile formed in recognition of Michael's hand holding his. He looked up at the grave face with concern.

"Smile, Michael—it is so long since I saw you smile with no beard."

He closed his eyes for a moment to fix that face in his mind's eye for easy recall. He wanted never to forget it. When the lips touched his brow, he opened his eyes again. Michael's smell was sweet, like those of men long at sea, their skins salted and never foul. Michael had bathed.

"Rest," said Michael. "I will get you some tea and broth cook has had steaming some days for you. 'Tis bound to be so thick you'll need a bloody knife to cut it!"

Alan fell into a pleasant languor until Michael returned. He found himself too weak to push up against the pillows, but he was not truly certain it was not because he wanted Michael's strong arms to help him.

While sipping his tea after having finished almost all of the rich broth under Michael's insistence, Alan found his imagination caught by the stocky figure centering the cabin. The shoulder-length hair, the fancy mustache, the more fanciful doublet thoroughly covered by exquisite embroidery and with sleeves slit to show the whiteness of the singlet beneath. The colorful pantaloons, the high boots and, above all, the doleful eyes were beyond belief. He stared rudely.

"You do not remember me, Alan?"

Alan began shaking his head—never in his life had he come across a being like this. But then the roaring Welsh laughter triggered a memory of kindness on the quay in Bristol, eight years earlier. He could almost taste the bread and cheese again.

"Henry!" he gasped. The pealing laugh was good to his ears.

"Aye, the same. Only 'tis my surname people know now—Morgan! The wig is enough to change any man's appearance." He seemed exasperated as he yanked it off and showed the springy, close-cropped hair. "Alan, never think of wearing a wig; the blasted things hold the heat of the day." He shook his head sadly. "But if 'twas not for Landon here just about putting a pistol ball in my fatted belly, you would have been left behind. Never would I have recognized you! Someone as ill as you is not for a vessel, 'tis not safe. But when he said your name and I took sight of you, I could not leave you."

73

Morgan studied Michael for an instant. "'Tis a strong love this man has for you, Alan, to be brave enough to threaten the life of Henry Morgan. I go not for this queer love, but 'tis not far from understanding. He has not left your side for a moment."

Michael's fair complexion was touched with color by the remark, and he flushed as Alan said, "I shall be in debt to him forever. Only months have I known him, yet I know of no man who has brought so much life to me. But stay," he switched back to Henry. "Do you know of Malcolm who came from Bristol with us?"

Henry let out another rolling laugh. "Aye, Alan. 'Tis quite a man this Malcolm, though strange. He speaks little, silently looking under his brow enough to make a man wonder if he is prattling like a woman. One day, if Malcolm learns to stand erect instead of falling back like about to thrust a stiff pego in cleavage, he would be most commanding in appearance. Between us, 'tis my thought he has fared best. I must credit him handsome, though his cheeks be sunken more than I like to see in a man, yet 'tis a thing better than the jowls I be getting, his lips out like a child being chastised for a misdeed yet showing defiance... this lends a peculiar handsomeness." Henry looked off in deep thought and then down at Alan's and Michael's clasped hands. 'Tis a most odd thought," he ended, looking directly at Alan.

"What, Henry?"

"If I were to have a liking to bed with a man, it would be Malcolm. His look and stance are of a constant challenge, which makes him much beset by others. And yet, beyond that blasted bosun and crew of our crossing, I would think him virginal in this aspect."

"He pursues wenches?"

Alan realized too late how the question had burst from his lips. Michael had looked down at their hands and was now searching his features. Alan wondered if his hand had tensed with his query.

Henry was filled with laughter: "He is *more* virginal with them!"

Alan forced a change in the talk because his thighs registered adjacent thickening and lengthening. "Would he be at Jamaica?" he asked.

"One never can know. 'Tis over a month since my departure. Malcolm signs on buccaneering vessels at the drop of a pistol ball. 'Tis reported he was capable beyond all men in a raid on Campeche. He does not stay on land for long. But you, Alan, will you stay in Jamaica?"

Alan looked at Michael to find an answer. "I do not know," he said after studying the steady gaze.

"It is an island much to my liking," said Henry. "I have a home there. If we can break the fever and fatten you up a bit, perhaps you would know your mind better." The ends of his mustache lifted as he beamed a smile. "There is time for that! For now, the quartermaster awaits me and I must go. He is dividing the spoils. It was a worthy raid! We managed 60,000 pieces of eight ransom for Santa Jago!"

In abrupt fashion, he turned about and left. Alan turned to Michael with some concern, which he found justified as Michael continued gazing steadily, questioningly.

"You have a love for this bloody Malcolm?" he finally asked. It was a sincere question without contempt or derogation intended.

Alan looked down at the hand he still clasped, the hand of the man who had awakened his spirit when he had thought it dead. He gripped it for a moment and then said, "Michael, a man can love more than one with equal heart, but he is most true to the one he is abed with."

The eyes maintained their gaze. Alan searched for clues, rediscovering Michael's handsomeness in his blond wavy hair, his smooth golden skin, his wide blue eyes and sensuous mouth. "Perhaps," Alan said, "you could understand if I were to say to you that were you, Malcolm and I in bed together, I would give as much as each wanted from me and the first of you with need would have me suck him dry in the sight of the other, so his passion in turn would be roused solidly for immediate taking."

"And if we were to fall to arguing on which is to be the first?"

"That would mean I would be hard pressed to take both, to put both in line so my tongue and lips could wrap about in a fashion to pipe your combined sources, fondly hoping your lips would be bonded in equal love which would provide me in unison."

Michael averted his gaze and scratched intently at the curly golden hair where the singlet gaped open on his chest: "You have set my bloody vitals on fire with the picture you have put in my mind!"

"I would drain your fire, Michael."

"But you talk of bloody orgies!"

"Even as you so strongly poured your passion into me in Santa Jago that first time, can you say that not for one fleeting moment there was not a thought of another love past?"

"You bloody well confuse me, Alan! Get your bloody bones under this cover and take rest!" He was forceful in tucking around Alan until only his head showed. "You have fever and talk in the heat of fever! You should bloody well get thoughts of sucking out of your bloody mind!" He latched on to Alan's beard and tugged. Alan found himself looking into the far reaches of a tropical sky. "You craze me enough to feel a madness in wanting to mount the bed and sink deep into your throat, to flood you at this very moment!"

With fists clenched at his sides, Michael strode to the cabin door and closed it quickly behind him.

"Michael?" Alan called out, but Michael was gone. "Oh, this bloody fever," he muttered half aloud, mimicking Michael. Exhausted, he closed his eyes and sought the blackness of sleep. It was a little while before the image faded, one of veiled gold above and below, with lush brown hair at the base of a flat abdomen which was advancing and receding so his inner throat could be stroked with a rock-hard cock. Later, he did not awaken but only smiled in his sleep when his hand shifted onto the puddle of hair above his navel.

"No, Mama Luke! No!" Alan cried out against the bitter brew forced between his lips. He screwed his eyes tightly when he turned his head away, finding comfort in the soft had that had been under his head but was now beneath his cheek. There was a dismaying weakness barely permitting his body to hold his lax joints together. The hand against his cheek felt warm. Alan discovered the fever had left him.

"You need to take more of this witch's brew."

Not only the sound of his voice, but his eyes also told Alan that he was not at the Wilson plantation. He was in a bed, a luxurious bed, in a bright and cheerful room with white plastered walls and neat curtains at the window. He slipped his head against the smooth hand and looked at the man next to the bed. He was close and his other hand was still poised with a mug of steaming brew.

"Would you take more? You have to, for a few days. It appears your fever has been broken with this amazing infusion. We must not risk the fever returning. Come!"

Alan accepted a few more sips while taking his eyes from the other hand and ugly brew to examine the face. There was intelligence there and a merry twinkle in the blue eyes. The brown hair had highlights and the tanned skin attested to exposure to the sun. The face was not exceptional otherwise and could not be said to be particularly handsome, though also not plain. Alan wondered how he could feel so weak and yet capable of having one length of flesh filling with strength.

"Who are you and where am I?" asked Alan. "Is this your home?"

The other took his time, first setting the mug on a small table and then rolling the sleeves of his singlet. Alan noticed the ripple of muscles under the fine, light brown hair of the arms. The hands were soft and the muscles were strong. That was always a pleasing combination; too bad the hair was not thicker, to be even denser than Michael's. It was also short hair. The opening of the singlet gaped wide for an instant and Alan quickly lowered his eyes to the exposed chest. The same brown hair was concentrated over the center of the chest in short whorls—each nipple would probably be ringed with it. Alan's strength began solidifying.

"I'm Hallet. Giles Hallet. A ship's surgeon I be and no, this is not my house. We received a battering from a Spanish vessel which opened fire for no apparent cause. Our damage being extensive, we took flight not to chance a return attack. We both stay with my colleague who is a physician here in Jamaica, in Port Royal. He was kind enough to have me here while our ship is careened on the beach and they make repairs."

He had spoken easily in a flowing style, slowly, seeming to run one sentence into the next. "Have I missed anything?" he asked when Alan looked puzzled.

"But how did I get here?" Alan wondered whether Morgan's ship had fallen under attack.

"Captain Morgan had you brought here. There is a man the likes of which I have never seen. In asking, he commands. He asked if I could tend to you."

Alan found his own smile spreading in response to the smile Hallet showed. "I seem to have much to thank him for," he said. "Will he be coming around?"

"But he has been!" Hallet wrinkled his brow. Alan obviously remembered nothing of the times he had struggled out of delirium to carry on what seemed coherent conversation. "He has gone off, his vessel having joined Captain Coxon's fleet for a raid on the Honduran coast."

The news saddened Alan. His thanks would have to wait for Morgan's return. "And Michael Landon?"

"He has gone with Morgan. There, too, is a singular man," said Hallet with conviction. He eyed Alan gravely and stated, "You did him a grievous

79

wrong. He understood it was fever, but scars in a man's heart develop from unmeant wrongs. It was sad to see, for he is highly devoted to you. I have never seen love so strong."

"But what could I have done?"

"In the depths of fever, you cried out for Malcolm, over and over again. Poor man. He spent many hours sitting by your side, waiting for that moment when you would realize he was there. When that moment arrived, it took two of us to pull him off you for fear he would snap your neck with his shaking of you. You see, at that moment you called him Malcolm and he could not convince you that he was Michael."

Utter dismay seared through Alan. "Oh my God," he cried. "He knows I love them equally, though differently. But to have called him by Malcolm's name is the worst of all."

"He was most aggrieved when we got him away from you. I took him to my chamber where he broke the feeling inside him with a rush of tears. I have seen men so handsome of build cry in pain or frustration in battle, but I have never seen one so torn by a hurt to his love." Hallet watched Alan's struggle briefly before saying, "I need to speak the truth with you. In consoling his misery, I…" He turned his head away; he could not look at Alan directly when he said, "If it were not for you confusing names, I would not have learned how loveable he is."

Hallet looked at Alan quickly. "You need have no fear. Our paths may never cross again and it took place only because he was so lost to himself."

Alan thought through Hallet's comments. "It

pleases me to know it happened," he confessed. "To have come so soon after suffering a hurt like I inflicted, perhaps he will feel free to partake of his pleasures instead of refraining because of me."

Alan took another appraisal of Hallet before saying, "If our positions were changed, with you I would have done the same."

Warmth returned to Hallet's eyes and he avoided further comment by assuming a professional air, taking hold of Alan's chin. "It's time we gave you some attention," he said as he began a critical examination. "Your skin has been damaged by a peculiar infection. We had to shave you to get rid of your vermin. It also eased when we swabbed you with strong tea."

"'Tis a relief not to be bearded." Then it struck him. "Tea?"

"It toughens the skin," Hallet explained, amused by Alan's consternation. "The most tender of skin can be made like a hide with enough of it but do not fear— I apply only enough to do good. Some of the inflamed areas have lessened, but it is not doing more than that." Hallet touched along Alan's cheek.

"I have seen cases where strange afflictions acquired in the tropics have disappeared in cold climates."

"Then I shall return to England," said Alan with determination. The tropics had brought nothing but problems to him.

Hallet reached for the cloth and the solution of tea on the table. "I would be willing to speak to our captain for you. We do not carry passengers, but since I have been attending you it would seem wise to be on

81

a ship with a surgeon." He began swabbing Alan's face.

"I cannot pay my passage until I reach England, but would pledge it if you are in a position to advance the amount."

Hallet continued dabbing with the cloth and said nothing until he had finished with the face and neck.

"We shall see what we can arrange," he said, setting the bottle on the table again. "Now let us continue with the rest of you," he said as he expertly drew off the covers. "Your sack of bones needs a good swabbing."

"What have you done," Alan demanded when he saw how far his ribs protruded.

"I told you we had to shave you to get rid of the vermin. We were able to stifle those on your head with oil and wrappings and it may be that we can save that. It may be that we have to shave that, if we cannot subdue the infection."

"But my hair—*all* my hair." Hastily he felt about his testicles. "Even from my bollocks!"

Hallet smiled, a smile filled with understanding for one who did *not* understand.

"It will grow! All too soon, Alan."

He let his hand glide over Alan in a wipe over the testicles, pressing the cock against the abdomen and then up to the chest to travel from one side to the other.

"I would be most distressed to have as much as you had."

In a fast sweep, his hand caught hold of Alan's cock, shifted the skin upward and then slid over the vivid cockhead. In the next move, his hands yanked the opening of his singlet wide.

"This, Alan, is enough at times to have made me want to sweep it off with a razor!"

Alan stared at the small clump and tried to picture it missing, the chest truly bared. He forced his gaze upward and locked their eyes.

"No!" he uttered, aghast. "You would not! 'Tis what a man is made of. 'Tis his strength!" He glanced at his body. "See how I am naked, left equal to a baby? I would want more than I had!"

"Alan?" Hallet waited until he had his attention. "A woman wears long skirts and shows her ankle with the promise that she will be as naked when her skirts are removed. A man goes about in breeches, his chest and legs haired; he promises to remove his breeches but remains near as covered as before. Does he truly give himself?"

With the lightest touch he returned to gliding his hand over Alan's body. Alan did not see the hand. He watched his cock bolt upward and begin a steady beat. Bared, he suddenly recalled how it used to rear that way in his youth, without a deceptive mask, and how so many times a day he could not resist mercilessly whipping that length until his body jerked and writhed in painful dry orgasms.

"You see?" Hallet continued. "You see, Alan, how your senses are aroused now that you are truly naked?"

"'Tis but the softness of your hand!" Alan denied. Alan concentrated… yes, it was the cook with the stiff knee, coming out of Bristol, who had stripped him in the galley and idolized his smooth flesh, touching, skimming, gliding over the hairless torso, never touching the cock that kept angling higher and higher and which, strained beyond reason, suddenly erupted with thick splattering smacks. Hallet was edging on Alan in the same way and his words held truth.

"Watch, Alan, watch!" he was saying. "Is it just the softness of my hand or is that I touch flesh which has not been touched for years?" Hallet checked the widening flare of Alan's cockhead. The skin was shining, glistening where fluids were pouring over. Hallet's eyes narrowed.

"Alan, I could stroke your body and have your prick become a fountain," he said, confirming what Alan knew. "I would not waste it."

Alan pushed to his elbows and grabbed at the peaking and throbbing fabric of Hallet's pantaloons. He was draining himself of strength and worked desperately until he paused to gaze at the living redness above his fist. He began struggling to bring himself closer.

"Stay, Alan!" Hallet commanded. "Do not exert yourself! As it is, I cannot help but exhaust you… you are near shaking!"

He made one pass and had the cock head glistening evenly. He drew the skin back harder and watched the new fluids come cascading over the tip, which darkened even more. No longer was he the surgeon with a patient and pushed Alan back so he could rest against the pillows without losing his hold or interrupting his urgent massage of Hallet's upright cock.

Alan shuddered as the warm lips closed over his head, ever increasing his coverage until he paused with throat filled and began playing his throat muscles in a manner which set Alan's body twisting.

Alan struggled with his closed hand as vitality entered the cock he held. A convulsion gripped him and his hand responded with a sudden jerk. The heavy flight from the crimson cockhead threw Alan into a paroxysm that ripped with such violent agony he wished it would never stop.

Chapter Nine

It was a bitter day in the middle of January 1660, when the ship reached Bristol. Hallet was unable to convince Alan he should await debarkation in the shelter of the cabin instead of in the driving rain on the deck. Alan was too exhilarated to heed the advice. Under Hallet's care he had thrived: His face had lost the gaunt look and flesh now covered his bony frame under his regrown hair, though he still appeared thin.

Alan felt to be his former self, a man of robust energy and fortitude. Hallet appeared to have been correct, for as soon as the ship had reached cool weather, the maddening itch in Alan's skin had begun to subside. Much to Hallet's relief, so did the itching of his own skin. No longer would he upset Alan as he had when he had painstakingly shaved off every hair in an attempt to squelch the itch and also to make his own nakedness equal to Alan's, nor would Alan ever upset him by remarking, "The only merit is that it has lent marvelous size to your pego and purse!"

Alan was assured his letter sent by another vessel before their departure had reached home. When the carriage door halted at the steps, his parents threw open the door as though they had been waiting for days. A thousand questions were streaming before

Alan could emerge and throw his arms around his mother. She had always been a small creature, but nine years of separation had made her seem tinier than he remembered. In the manor, for each question there seemed to develop two more. Alan compromised by condensing his sordid story into chronological form, leaving out details—like the floggings—to save his mother's feelings.

Even so, she had some strong words Alan never realized she had known and she applied them to the maltreatment of her son. These caused Alan to examine his own attitudes and, even though he was far away from there, he found his heart was carrying a deep hatred for the Wilsons and for the Spaniards. Later that evening, sitting before the fireplace in a comfortable chair and gazing into the flames, warmed by them and by Hallet's close presence, his mind clouded frequently. Henry felt speechless when Alan announced, "I should return to join Henry and help raid those blasted Spaniards!"

"Your first day home and you speak thus?"

Hallet had voiced his surprise while still recovering from Alan's shocking declaration.

Alan looked over at Hallet and let his tongue slip between his parted lips until he could flick it over the upper lip, always inciting Hallet's sensuality in this manner. Hallet was already trapped.

Any remembrance of Malcolm brought licentious thoughts, his backward tilt inviting Alan to masturbate until he threw his sperm the length of the body and, while it flowed downward, to drain Malcolm's cock between hollowed cheeks. Michael brought lubricious thoughts, his hard, shiny cock being for endless sucking, becoming flaccid only when both agreed they had had enough. But Hallet brought lecherous thoughts: As a surgeon he knew how every inch of a body could respond. Hallet had developed Alan's spermatic resources beyond that of which Alan thought any man capable. With satisfaction, Alan had turned the techniques on Hallet, the tongue and the lips snarling Hallet's thoughts while his groin developed a pounding.

"I'll not be returning there while you still be around," Alan confessed, "lest you go with me."

Hallet launched his hand over testicles and cock to denote his arousal before saying, "I'm willing to set up practice on this spot! In fact, with you being my first patient here, I'll be advising you that it's time to retire. Mind you, not for your health, but because you do not keep your tongue civil! You know well what that does to me…" Hallet nudged his crotch and got his stiffness outlined by the fabric.

Alan made his tongue become more obvious by playing over the upper and lower lips simultaneously. Safely shielded by the chair, he whipped open the slit of his breeches and let his straining red cockhead show.

"Mrs. Steele!" Hallet called out loudly instead of using the quiet voice. "Your son still needs rest and I request your permission to withdraw."

His eyes roved over Alan hastening to cover himself before he added, "And I too feel the need for rest. This excitement of homecoming, your superb meal and Mr. Steele's excellent wines have made me ready to sleep where I sit."

Mrs. Steele fluttered with sudden energy: "I must prepare the bed-warming pans—oh dear!"

"We'll do it, Mother. Do you still keep it next to the fireplace in my room?"

Alan's bed needed no warming that evening. Hallet grabbed him the instant the door was closed and threatened, "I'll teach you to rouse me in front of your parents! I shall titillate your bollocks without mercy! I shall run my tongue into those sensitive spots until you throw over all the linens! Explain *that* to your mother in the morning!"

"'Tis you I would blame. I would tell her you did it, that you always hand yourself. Now, will you kindly take your claws off me?"

Hallet pulled away with astonishment. Alan's tone had been terribly cold, demanding.

Alan broke into a coy smile as he said, "'Tis every piece of clothing I wish to remove so your tongue finds no obstacle!"

Hallet held true to his word and set Alan thrashing in short order. Hallet's own security collapsed as Alan turned about and set his tongue in like attack, duplicating Hallet's movements within a second of onset. Their ardors pitched as their actions intensified. Alan could feel evidence of his extreme excitement in the rigidity extending to the very root inside him. Like Hallet, vibrantly stiff in angry color about a gaping orifice opened wide for the heavy burst that was about to come, Alan had followed suit, developed by observation. He suddenly gasped and pulled himself slightly away.

For the first time, Hallet's lips were bottomed deep within Alan's heavy black hair. A shattering impulse began racing through Alan and his lips glided in haste down Hallet's length. He tried using his throat muscles like Hallet but barely had he constricted than they were pushed back by an expanding wedge and he felt the hurtling force being released. He pinned his arm tightly over Hallet's back and rammed violently into the depths of his throat.

When they had extinguished the candle and were nestled closely under the heavy quilts, exhausted, Alan's voice took on great concern.

"You keep clearing your throat," he said. "Are you developing a cold?"

"It's your blasted hair!" Hallet replied, sounding outraged. "I've been picking it from my teeth and mouth and yet find that there's more in my *throat*!"

Alan suppressed a rising giggle while Hallet continued to struggle with his problem. Impulse had Alan open his mouth and restraint silenced him. If he were to have Hallet recall the weeks without such annoyance, Hallet would be pestering again.

Alan snuggled closer to compress the barrier between them and he passed his hand along Hallet's form until it was buried in the pubes. If there was only some way to let Hallet know that Alan's appetite was whetted when Hallet was denuded. Alan worked his fingers but could not feel the flesh through the mass of hair. He vividly recalled how that bared skin had excited him, Hallet's cock looking so majestic, its smooth flesh merging with that of the body. Resolutely, he silenced himself. Hallet would be persistent and Alan never again intended to give up his own lush cover.

It was Alan who set to coughing the next day, and Hallet's fears about Alan's inconsiderate exposure to cold and rain were confirmed by late afternoon.

Throughout the day his accusations were cast aside by Alan, who kept insisting it was only a slight cold. It was Alan, though, who finally became meek and admitted he was feeling very poorly. Hallet became furious when he felt Alan's brow and quickly set his ear on Alan's chest.

"After all your body has fought, it would take something like this to finish you off in short order!" Hallet cried out vehemently as he helped Alan to his room. "In such poor health, you had the gall last night to be thinking of taking revenge on the Spaniards!"

Hallet's life in the next days became a nightmare. He was desperate and uncertain about what to do. Alan's fever was as though a baking fire had been stoked in his head and was boiling every bit of moisture out to the surface of his body. His skin under the hair had turned splotchy, a burning red. The only course Hallet could think to pursue was the treatment for smallpox and he poked about the fireplace until it blazed well and the heat in the room became near suffocating. He kept not only the windows closed tightly, but the bed curtains drawn as well. He plied Alan with cordials to make him sweat even more, and considered letting some blood. He theorized that once and for all, the fevers and infection had to be cleared out and that there was no better way than through sweat and blood.

When Alan, in delirium, began clawing his skin and breaking through with his fingernails, Hallet obtained mittens and secured them with cord at the wrists. He knew well what Alan was going through; some of the fever had touched him and the itching of Hallet's skin had become maddening. He ignored his own safety and tended Alan through day and night.

91

Hallet had given no great thought to some of what he observed—it was not too unusual with raging fevers and was invariably temporary. It became fully unusual the day Alan reached the point of sleeping peacefully once again. Hallet took advantage of the opportunity to tend to his own needs and, with a basin and cloth, began bathing his own body, which had been neglected through all that time. His fever had been only slight, but the evidence was on the cloth and he scrubbed all the harder. A look of horror spread across his face, not for himself but for Alan.

Each passing minute was lessening Hallet's time for debate. Alan's movement's showed signs that the crisis was well past. Action was needed more than debate. He put Alan's mother on guard for the difficult time that would be coming.

Hallet could not forgive himself in the next few days for not having bathed Alan in darkness: When the covers were drawn back, Alan began going into shock—the linens were black with fallen hair. When the scrubbing cloth began wiping his skin clean, Alan's eyes rolled upward, staring and rarely blinking. In a way, it simplified Hallet's task, providing him with a limp, unresisting body on which to work. Hallet proceeded swiftly, the sense of discovery making him anxious about the new quality of Alan's skin. While a penis is enshrouded with skin softer and smoother than any other part of a man's body, smoother even than a woman's skin, Alan had acquired the same texture all over his body and limbs. Hallet checked under his own singlet: He had not been distinctly aware that his had also softened in texture, though not as much as Alan's. With wonderment, he began on Alan's head: The clumps of long, black hair were separating from the scalp as though there had never been roots. As a surgeon he had faced many difficult sights, but this one shook him deeply.

Force-feeding was Hallet's only means of getting sustenance into Alan, him spooning broths and letting them trickle down the throat, ever hopeful that his timing was right and swallowing would take place between breaths. During feeding, Hallet kept the covers turned down. While waiting for the trickling down from the last spoonful to cease, he would survey Allan: A new sense of beauty was emerging under Hallet's gaze.

Alan was still thin, but his body was well proportioned and, fully denuded as Hallet had always wished him to be, it was an exciting body. Because of Alan's height, his long legs were not at all stocky; they were slender, without bony knees and tapering to slender ankles. The face—allowing for the fixed stare—had all its handsomeness exaggerated by the shiny pate. Even the lack of eyebrows forced attention to the fine features. In Hallet's eyes, Alan was becoming an exhilarating beauty.

Distracted as he was that day, wishing the long cock he had been admiring would become filled with life again, his timing went wrong and Alan gagged. The body struggled while the eyes bulged in their stare. The lids snapped shut and the coughing began. Hallet forced Alan's head over the side of the bed and lowered it; Alan was coughing in earnest.

"You bloody bastard!" Alan muttered slowly, still gasping. "You tried to drown me!" Gagging coughs became interspersed with pouring sounds. Every ounce of broth he had consumed was lost and when the retching stopped he collapsed against the pillow, breathing deeply.

Hallet ignored the eyes which would not let him out of sight after he cleaned the mess from the floor. When he began applying the pomade of calf's-foot oil and veal broth, as he had been doing daily, Alan kept his eyes tightly closed and, through clenched teeth, vowed revenge, muttering, "'Tis every one of the bloody bastards I'll kill! Every last one! I am going back, Hallet. I am going back to kill every Spaniard I can lay my hands on! I am going to kill that bastard Wilson and his like! He may have ruined my arse, but he'll never again shit when I finish with him! Those bloody bastards!"

Hallet endured the outbursts for days. Conscientiously, he had increased pomading to twice daily and, twice daily, Alan ranted. Where Hallet became aroused to dripping rigidity in working the pomade, until it became absorbed, Alan was only reminded of his loss. It was becoming an agonizing torture to Hallet and he finally reached his breaking point, spitting out his words viciously.

"You can 'bloody bastard' them all you want!" he cried out. "What's to gain from it? My hands are near shaking when they touch your body! My prick aches for its need of you! But no—we have only a creature without a soul who seeks nothing but revenge! Is that all that matters to you? With that worthless hair, so went your love for me? Is it that you will raise your prick only to ream out Wilson's bum?"

Hallet's chest was heaving with emotional exertion. He glared, balanced on the line between love and hate. "Stare, blast you!" he continued, yanking his singlet upward. "It befits a man dead in his body!"

94

Hallet threw the singlet aside; his voice was agonized as he said, "I shall let you stare at a man who lives!"

He began unfastening his belt; kicking aside his breeches, Hallet groaned from his hand's touch about the stiff shaft.

"Alan, stare at its hardness—it is near painful! Just so," he exclaimed, "twice a day I have pumped, yet at night next to you it becomes hard as ever. This bareness we have drives a prick searching for roughness and it finds none!"

Alan's thoughts jumbled. *From the chin up and the testicles down, Hallet appeared unscathed, though his chest and abdomen were now bare. It was odd. It was different, it was...*

"Alan!" Hallet tried to establish the sternest of tones, but realized his failure when he heard the quaver in his own voice. "I have stayed at your side like a faithful dog all through your illness. I tried my best and even took on your malady. I have not failed in one sense." He took a sharp breath. "I find myself more devoted to you than ever! Look at my prick— look at it, Alan! It is hardened near bursting with my need for you... for your love!" Hallet's hand was swift in catching hold of Alan's genitals. His voice turned jagged as he said, "If you do not face love, then I leave this room for the last time!"

Alan was moved. Revenge was uppermost in his mind, yet the pathetic sight of Hallet begging for rightfully due affection began an upheaval that was like the birth of a new volcano. He reached for his own muscled thigh and passed his hand along the depleted hair. Why had he not been able to retain even that much? *Bare! Totally bare! Bloody Wilson! Bloody*

95

Spaniards! He would… he heard the choking sob and looked into the moist eyes. In a rapid move, he pulled Hallet to the bed.

When Alan began holding Hallet, his consolation was melancholy. Vaguely he was aware of the softness of the skin against him and where his hands were stroking. He was even more aware of the moist warmth of Hallet's lips, how avidly they were being applied to his neck and shoulder. There was a new tenderness mixed with fervor. Had Hallet's love multiplied because of his nakedness? The head was shifting. Light stubble on Hallet's chin grazed a nipple. In quick response it rose, craving encircling lips. The hand skimming smoothly along his body stopped over hardened flesh. The lips were moving lower, leaving a trail from the tongue. Alan suddenly caught Hallet up and their mouths met in merciless pressure. Between them, two cocks were pinned side by side.

"I refused you the other day," Alan interrupted as he forced Hallet away. "Turn the mirror about: I would see myself."

Hallet straddled Alan on hands and knees; it would be just as well, he reasoned. Another two seconds against that satiny skin would have brought inundation. Slowly he raised to his knees, his cock following, throbbing and pointing upward, spilling fluid. He waited a moment more and control was his.

The image in the mirror was startling to Alan. The play they had undergone required that he put his first attention on the reflection of his groin and his vision was filled with the sight of a cock which was almost frightening against the bareness around it, its length appearing so much greater. Below it the testicles hung heavily… Alan wondered whether they had always been so large, or whether they had gained capacity to meet Hallet's demands He turned for a side view and watched the nearly horizontal prick beat in the struggle to support the weight—the bulging midpoint was exaggerated and now it could be seen that there was equal narrowness at the base and behind the flare. Never had Alan studied past reflections, using them erotically to speed orgasm; now for the first time he discovered the immensity of the head, the flare seeming so great for the narrowness behind it. The heavy vein along the shaft ran all the way back to the base. Pressures mounted within him and the shaft pulled up to horizontal, the tip increasing in size as it darkened.

Hallet dared not say a word to interrupt this study. He watched Alan flatten his hand on the lean belly and began shifting it upward. Hallet tensed: Recollections of the texture there had him in a state of anticipation. Alan was also responding; his cock jerked upward to full hardness in one move. Hallet was gripping his thighs in his fight to keep from bursting. When Alan said, "Giles, will you come here?" Hallet moved rapidly and, for all his wishing it would be so, was unprepared for Alan's clutching hands, which pulled their bodies close. His wet cockhead skidded up Alan's smooth body and became smothered by the flesh pressed about it.

All the while Alan had been staring at the mirror, Hallet's excitement had been intensifying. Now it was blasting a tunnel between them. His body jerked with each coughing groan; the wetted skin was beyond smooth and brought heavy throbs that he tried to still with more pressure. Barely had he shifted position when the shooting fluid raced up between them. Abstention had advantage in quality, but early release brought frustration.

Alan kept his arms locked around Hallet long after the last shudders had died. A steady tingling radiated from Alan's testicles and his lips parted more than usual; his eyes lost their focus, gazing well beyond the confines of the room. Was his nakedness total disaster? With only a pair of breeches, nobody would suspect how bare he was; with a wig he could be presentable. With nothing, he was being loved; their cocks were still stiff, hard, beating. Alan discovered that Hallet's hands had been roaming. They were just coming up over the thighs, and continued up his sides and into his armpits. Reflex made Alan thrust his hips forward, his soaking cock about to jam up under Hallet's ribs. Those hands were now descending down his back, over newly sensitized buttocks, slipping into the cleft. Alan buckled his knees slightly; fingers and hands were no longer veiled from contact by a furry pelt and he jerked his body upward, letting the fingers slip farther.

The hand behind and the lubricated cock to the fore set Alan to humping. His muscles began betraying him and his erratic movements could not be anticipated. His cock felt so enormous, so hard; he rammed against Hallet and let the hot blast burst between them. He arched to show the tip, letting ensuing bursts hurtle and fall back to their chests, coving the flowing cockhead. The strength needed to hold himself still during the shattering bursts deserted him and he shook violently and collapsed against Hallet.

"Giles!" Alan whispered a minute later. "If we stay

so, I find myself mad enough to try again immediately. I would throw the soft sweetness on your back while my arms and hands lavish attention on your front!"

Hallet did not answer, except to confirm his own pleasure by sliding side to side against Alan. He turned his head to look at their images. This time Alan was gazing steadily at the strange appearance of his head. Hallet shifted away slightly and Alan's cock shifted out of entrapment, vibrantly stiff, heady headed with vivid color under the white glaze.

Later, cleaned and sprawled on the chair before the tilted mirror, Alan stared at his reflection for a long time. He broke the silence by saying, "Giles, it is an ugly sight, though one a person could accept."

Hallet smiled fondly and said, "I have, Alan. You are not the man who was beneath the encumbrance; you are the man I would pleasure from dawn through to the next if you would but allow me."

Alan tried to comprehend what Hallet saw. Could his love be only for those genitals which had become so prominent? But then there was also the deep-set navel, the fold over the top like a sensuous, drooping eyelid. And there were those two large discs on his chest, centered with brazen nipples. His body was exciting without the screening blackness, even for its thinness. But the face? The features were there, gaunt but with overpowering impact, his brown eyes rich looking, his teeth glistening behind parted lips enriched in color by the lovemaking they had experienced.

No, if his cock had been able to rise to near perpendicular under this scrutiny, it was no disaster. He passed his hand down his front until he reached the fully vertical prick, and it was as fine an experience to touch the satiny shaft as to encircle the only soft skin he had ever had.

"Perhaps others may also find me tolerable," he suggested.

"One is not enough?" Hallet retorted immediately. "Can you never be satisfied? There must be others—do you spurn my love?"

Alan reached back and grabbed Hallet's wrists. "'Tis only a fool who speaks so," he said, "and never have you been one. I speak of my parents, the townsfolk and of others I may encounter. I would be well satisfied to stay in this room forever and only have you suck to your heart's content! Nay, to soak in our spunk and replenish without cease!"

"Suck, is it? Soak, is it? I speak of love!"

"Then love me!"

Alan released the wrists and the hands began skimming along the chest until Hallet was bent sufficiently to touch pursed lips to Alan's head. His skin tingled where the hands had touched and a flush of color crowned the cock's flaring head.

"I would not have believed anyone capable so soon," came Hallet's voice, filled with surprise. "I be in a most awkward position and need to get on the floor between your legs."

Alan looked up at the mirror and their eyes locked. Slowly he spread his legs wide and said, "See—you speak of love but only want to suck my passion from me!"

Alan ducked his head to the side as Hallet lunged over his length to grab. His testicles were shifting upward a second after Hallet's hand blurred with motion.

Chapter Ten

"You're blind, Alan! You're *blind*!" Hallet's voice was nearly at a screaming pitch. He went back to pacing rapidly about the room.

Alan was very calm as he repeated, "'Tis that I must." He watched the lengthened pace for a moment and added, "'Tis sorry I am, Giles, but 'tis the way I feel. No one has any right to deliver injustice to a human as he well pleases."

Hallet stopped in his tracks and pointed an accusing finger. "Hah! And what have you been saying? How did you find the right in wanting to return to the Indies and kill off the Spaniards or the Wilsons?"

"'Tis for what they did," Alan answered directly, expecting this to represent full justification.

Hallet dropped into the chair facing Alan and leaned forward, pointing. He was shaking the finger ominously. "For a whole blasted year you've enjoyed the company of people who have fully accepted you. Damn you, you've even had the gall to stop wearing the periwig!"

"'Tis too hot a thing, as Morgan complained."

Hallet's face flushed and his voice became louder. "You have the audacity to look at me squarely and claim it is because the wig gets too hot?" The flush which had disappeared when he placed the question bloomed again when Alan nodded his head.

"You bastard! You know damned well that has nothing to do with it! You've come to like your nakedness so much that you want everyone to see it! Next you'll be going about with no clothes!"

He bolted from the chair to begin pacing again.

"Try a wig and see," said Alan.

Hallet stopped, befuddled, then returned to his pacing.

"Giles, 'tis most grateful I am to you for being so wonderful a guardian, but my mind drives me to save others... no other choice comes to mind. How I shall do it is not yet certain. To join Henry and his buccaneers would be one way, but I feel I must be the master of it, not a servant."

Hallet traipsed to the chair. He closed his fist and began chewing on his bent index finger while staring at Alan. In reviewing the past year, a thought flashed through his mind.

"Alan!" he called as he stopped his gnawing. "Tell me one thing: All these lessons in swordsmanship— were they for this goal?"

Hallet's spirit sank as Alan replied, "Yes."

"But they have done wonders for you. All the other things as well have built you up to the point where I find it difficult to sleep with you. Though you exhaust me, I find I cannot wrap myself closely enough or feel enough of that body, which has become like one I have never seen.

"In clothing, you set the women in a swoon... no, don't try to deny it, for you well know."

Hallet's smile twisted, a little bitter.

"I have watched many a first introduction where their eyes open wide if you are in a wig and wider if you are not. But I venture that less than five seconds pass before those very eyes are divesting you of every bit of cloth covering your flesh, taking you down to what I know is that bare body that even I know sets me aflame with desire."

"Any man can build his body, Giles, and you know it. You, not quite handsome in features as most people think, need only do as I did and you would have the same attention. Features are one thing, but bodies mean pleasure and everyone has that interest. You really should develop your body, you know."

Hallet paled and his voice carried no strength: "You are no longer interested in me, are you Alan?"

Alan was too casual when he said, "Now Giles, you know I have great love for you. I was only placing in reverse what you have been saying.

"We get nowhere with this discussion. 'Tis once again I say I intend to return there and take a revenge—if you must have some type of excuse for it, so that another youth who may sail in pursuit of fortunes in the Indies will not fall into the type of hell I did."

Underneath, Hallet's pot had been set to boiling. In skimming from the surface he said, "You have become no better than they if you wish to impose harm on them; you have as little use for humanity as they do. You want to kill to prove that, as with perverse pleasure, everything has to be as you wish it." He had caught the first bubble from the boil and the surface disrupted. "That young man! For all I know, there have been others behind my back as well!"

103

"You speak folly," said Alan disdainfully, but he knew that to which Hallet referred.

Three days earlier he and Hallet had arrived in the stable with the intention of saddling up and riding off to enjoy the break of spring and its first day of warmth. Upon entering the stable, they surprised a youth who was positioned at the window. He had the gawkiness of a young man, but his singlet and loose breeches draped in a way they could only do on a good mature figure. When the fellow spun around with absolute fright, there was a moment when his very stiff cock, free of the hand which had been rubbing it, swung with a thud against his thigh and then began collapsing rapidly. His mouth was agape and his hands were flat against the wall to support him.

Alan gave a quick wink to Hallet, who was aware of Steele senior's adventures. "You expected Mr. Steele?" he asked.

The youth nodded his head, his mouth still hanging open, the red tip of the tongue frozen over his pale lower lip.

"Mr. Steele is… indisposed." Alan had paused to find the correct word. He did not feel it was appropriate to disclose that his mother had exceeded the dosage of a physic and that his father would be indisposed for at least a day, if not more.

"I shall see him another time." The youth's words fell over each other and he braced himself to flee.

Alan nudged Hallet and they both confronted him at close quarters.

"You would leave with your pego hanging out that way?"

The young man flushed brightly and closed his

eyes. His breath became shaking sobs as he felt Alan's hands close about the sides of his breeches and pull them from under his belt. As though accustomed to it, he lifted his arms high, eyes still tightly closed, while his singlet was pulled from his belt and then up and over his head. The buckle of his belt glinted as it caught the light from the stable door, flashing in accord with the heaving of his chest.

Hallet's eyes did not miss a single detail of the exposed body, but he felt it was no more than right to say, "You've given him a turn—let him be."

Alan turned to Hallet and winked. To the youth he said, "Tell me, boy! Were you waiting for my father to divest you and feast on your beauty?"

The mouth snapped shut, but the underlip was caught far under the teeth. The eyes were shut as tightly as they could ever be.

Alan gave a side-glance at Hallet. He was assured that Hallet found the young man as attractive as he did. He turned back and slipped his fingers under the belt; in his estimation the fellow could have worked for a miller, so broad were his shoulders. His features had a certain charm and his hair drooped over his brow enticingly, their light blond shades so different from the auburn crop below. Under the crop the youth hung fairly, his parts held well forward. If Alan knew his father well enough, this one would be one of his regular visitors. Although broad shouldered, his muscles were not evident and there was an alluring softness to his limbs and body.

"'Tis inappropriate, this belt," said Alan.

The young man's underlip, as far in as it was, seemed to be withdrawn farther.

Alan put his hands to work as soon as the belt dropped, gently closing about the other's hips. Gradually he slipped his hands upward until his thumbs rested on the nipples. He teased with his thumbs, but the youth had the kind that would not rise, though his other flesh filled with reaction in their stead.

"Could we replace my father?" Alan asked.

The underlip slipped out, glistening with saliva and marked where teeth had been pressing hard. His large eyes opened and started at Alan for a moment before glancing downward. He discovered that Alan's breeches were no longer draped flat and looked back at Alan's face.

Hallet's voice did not seem to break the young man's gaze as he said, "Alan, come on—you've given him enough of a difficult time! I warrant he is a beauty, but enough is enough…" Hallet's voice trailed off; the youth was slowly nodding assent.

Alan kept his eyes steady, interfering only for the moment when he drew his singlet over his head. He exaggerated his movements as he kicked off his shoes. He intensified his stare and the young man slowly lifted one foot after the other from his own shoes and breeches.

"Hallet!" The voice was commanding. "You will make him feel uncomfortable if you remain so dressed."

When Hallet was with but belt and breeches, Alan stepped free of his. Slowly the youth's eyes began lowering; he never saw Alan's hand snake out to catch his wrist and sent him spinning toward the pile of hay.

The refreshment of a youth, glorying in capabilities still relatively new, set Hallet's heart to pounding as much as Alan's. His cries could have been heard as far as the house when he responded to the pair's experienced hands and tongues. He tried desperately to take Alan as he had Alan's father, but his jaws ached before he could cover the flare. It was of little consequence, as the unexpected encounter had Alan bring him to gagging and chocking in moments. With Hallet there was no problem; he was accommodated easily and the bursts were deep in the throat. In all, they had the youth four times before their fires dulled.

The young man seemed shattered as he sprawled over the hay, his abdomen so collapsed it would seem as though his spine should be showing. Alan had not failed to observe that through all the rapport, even when downing Hallet, the youth had not been without some form of contact with Alan. For Hallet, his service was efficient. For Alan, he forced delay, constantly returning to sucking and tonguing the hairless plain over the pubic bone in delightful torment.

Now, in this argument with Hallet, Hallet had picked on occasion to display jealousy. Hallet—the one who doubted that Alan could bring him to climax in fast sequence—was the one who had buried himself deeply in the young man's throat the third time without displaying any qualm about being able to inject heavily, not the fourth time when the youth had buttocks as a pinnacle when his mouth was low, this time past the head of Alan's cock.

"You speak folly!" Alan repeated with greater emphasis. "You accuse *me* of having folly, of being blind in my desire to seek revenge, yet you are no different from me."

107

Hallet had buried his face in his hands and was swaying in his chair. A deep hurt burst through Alan—he could not determine whether this was a hurt he felt for Hallet or for himself. He tried to make his voice as soft as he could when he said, "Giles, I have never gone behind your back. You say you have a love for me, but I wonder if it is as great as the one I have for you. You accuse me wrongly.

"If you refer to the stable lad, you partook of him as well as I. For that time there were three people who had no interest in anything but to pleasure each other. I have told you what I told Michael and I thought you understood: You are far more intelligent than he and I assumed that since you did not stalk out as he did, you knew well of what I spoke. 'Tis sorry I am if something as trivial as the two of us enjoying the spunk of youth has brought about difficulty."

Hallet uncovered his face slowly; it was expressionless. His voice held no emotion as he said, "Leave me be; away with you else there be disaster."

Alan reached out and then cut off the words that were forming. He did not bother putting on his singlet or shoes, but strode out only in his breeches.

Many things clotted Alan's mind as he slammed the door of the house and let his weight fall against it. He breathed as if he had undergone great exertion. He cursed Hallet, the Wilsons, the Spaniards and finally his parents for having brought him into this world. A whip could be formed not only of leather but of words, and the sting from words was deeper than any he had ever known from a lash. Angled as he was against the door, his eyes were caught by how his toes were curled under, biting into the ground. He glanced at his hairless legs and swore he would let everyone know of his misfortunes. Naked, he would mount a steed bareback and ride through the countryside with a "Fuck!" to the maiden who swooned.

"*God Almighty*," Alan swore as he stripped off his breeches and belt in the stable. "Take sight of this and let everyone see!" He had bent his knees and forced his hips forward so his stark genitals were wholly exposed.

"It is a sight to behold!"

Alan was jolted by the voice; there should have been no one here. Seductively peering about the pile of hay was the face of the youth. It was Alan who froze this time.

"I waited to see you yesterday, but you did not come. Today I saw you through the window as you came to the stable—you looked angry. I have already taken off my things lest you tear them in your anger."

Curiosity swamped all other feelings that had possessed Alan; he came around the hay.

"What have you done to yourself!" he exclaimed as he saw the figure stretched languorously on the hay with arms outstretched. The excitement filling his cock was enough to make him want to masturbate without taking another step.

"I admired you so much that I took my father's razor, since I do not yet own one myself."

Alan stared at the totally bared youth for only a moment before throwing himself on him. He began smothering him with the kisses he had hoped to place on Hallet when their argument had been dissipated. Slowly he came to realize that his outpouring was being returned with honesty.

He forced easement and then said, "You know, of course, how foolish you have been with the razor."

"Foolish?" The youth looked surprised and pushed Alan away from him and then said, "I dared not do my head, for my parents would have been most aggrieved."

Alan was stunned. His lips parted farther and he knew he was staring, but he remained speechless. The lad became concerned.

"'Twas not meant to upset you," he apologized. "I long to be as bare as you."

Alan found he could not face the eyes. He threw his arm about the youth, burying the sweet face between his shoulder and neck. He found himself confused. His heart beat out with the need to murder those who had wronged him, yet here was a mere youth having nothing but admiration for what they had done. Breaking with contriteness, Alan rocked their nearly bonded bodies and considered the young man. How could he possibly understand what Alan had gone through? He could not impose such a need on this young person. Alan's bodily needs, however, were replacing those of his mind.

He inched his way along the boy's neck until the arms began releasing them, allowing greater coverage. With full access, he followed Hallet's tactics and permitted his tongue to reach deep within the denuded armpit; the writhing against him fired him even more and he swept over the body until his saliva glistened in highlights over every part.

He dwelled on the sacrificial stubble as the youth had done with him; the lad seemed to have lost his senses and, with his arms along his sides, lay with his eyes closed and teeth biting hard into his underlip. Where Alan had been prompted to spear into his glistening belly, he only pleased himself flat with restraint and greater deliberation that began spreading heavier layers from his tongue.

He had left sensibilities so far behind that it was not until his tongue was again swashing across the belly that he realized the youth had already erupted. Alan hastened to even the spread before his violent throbbing climaxed. At the end he rammed hard against the belly as his lips sucked in those of the boy and his passion added stock to the wet coat on the young man.

An extra shudder ran through Alan as the youth slipped his hands over Alan's back. He was not willing to free the firmness of the lips he pressed. He wanted to consume them; their owner offered his tongue instead. Hungrily, Alan drew it in. All the time, he knew he had nothing more than a callow youth in his grasp, but no one had ever given himself so completely. He savored the tongue as long as he was permitted and then his lips were roaming over the face, down the cheeks and his tongue was prodding into the ears. All this time he also knew they were both throbbing below as strongly as ever. His breath was catching and he could no longer control where his lips were placed. Alan had begun working down to the throat when he was rolled on his back; the boy followed without losing contact.

Experience did not seem to be an essential in the unleashing; the young man was as voluptuous as Alan. He was maddening in his kisses from ear to brow to chin. In a sudden spurt, his knees were in Alan's armpits and his soaked cock was being forced past Alan's lips, his wet testicles surrounding Alan's chin when the cock reached depth in the throat. He withdrew suddenly and was again flat on him, totally given up to their orgy and desiring only to run his demanding cock against Alan. Their lips met and his tongue probed, mimicking the movements of his body and the tongue stabbed deep. When the lad stilled Alan, on his back, squirmed and thrust and almost instantly proved he could equal the love.

Alan drew in the sweet smell of hay past his partner's ear for the longest of times after they had rolled and Alan topped him. He knew he was a crushing weight, but could not find the energy to move off or resist the thrill of slipping within close confines. When he finally tried the boy hung on, so he stayed as did their erections, two throbbing cocks imprisoned by their bellies.

Alan was immediately reeling when he awoke with the burden on him. The boy was asleep and the light at the window was that of sunset. He had to awaken the boy, but he also wanted to spend the night this way. Alan moved his hips slightly and found the confines still soaked—it had not been any type of dream.

When the youth discovered the lateness of the hour and hurried into his clothing, his requests to meet Alan the next day weakened Alan all the more. He bid his farewell and then stretched out on the hay. His skin was nowhere near dry when Hallet appeared before him, feet braced wide and fists on his hips.

"Here lies the conqueror," he barked. "From the mess I would think it was the youth again."

Alan looked up at him lazily. He deliberated a moment and then said, "It was." Noisily, he began stroking his wet skin.

Hallet flushed badly: "You're like a harlot!" He turned suddenly and was gone into the twilight.

Alan did not care whether he had any supper—his mind was filled with the youth and of his own future. It was ridiculous, he thought, but here was just the kind of person who would be caught in adventure and meet death. Alan became more determined to make the world safe for these young people. Somehow, conviction was lacking; to love and to kill appeared to be the only goals and he wanted as much of both as he could get. His wet fingers felt good on the sensitive cock that valiantly struggled, willing to meet the challenge.

Chapter Eleven

The means of love were without lack for Alan; at times the youth, William Mead, made them debilitating.

The means for killing were not clear: The elder Mr. Steele had given downright refusal to the request for a sum to pay Alan's passage to the Indies. Of the alternate ways, Alan needed experience to be able to sign on as a seaman and he had no intention of chancing indenture again. One year began passing and his adventures remained restricted to the execution of passion. His cutlass was wielded in mighty strokes, and though it lacked an edge the hard and blunt tip laved bodies or filled guts with white fluid.

Hallet had given up Alan before the summer of 1661 and gone to London to set up a practice. His jealousy had made him leave in a huff: "You're free to suck on William now as much as you want!" was his departing remark. Later, reading between the lines of Hallet's first letter, Alan sensed regret for his action.

William Mead was at the Steele manor far more than at his own home, at first on the pretext of tutoring. He was welcomed into the house with no question and there were also no inquiries on that occasion when time seemed to have escaped them and

Mrs. Steele suggested William stay the night. Mr. Steele raised his eyebrow and Alan gave him a warning look: The message it conveyed was, "You say one thing and I will tell Mother you had him before I did!" After that, William became a frequent overnight visitor. Alan also found that the tutoring changed from a scam to an earnest endeavor. William seemed to absorb knowledge like a sponge; ever willing to learn and ever willing to play, he seemed to have no serious faults and Alan was delighted with him.

One fault seemed uncorrectable, even though Alan insisted that William restrict the razor to his face, where a light fuzz was developing into a beard. Twice that summer, however, the boy went all the way. Stern though he tried to be, Alan was pleased. The ritual had gained some meaning apart from the idolization of Alan. It meant that hands and mouths were not to get involved; they would alternately build the wash on their bodies until the last straining effort forced them into the oblivion of exhaustion and sleep. Unlike Hallet, and even though he capably maintained a high drain on Alan's reserves, William found pleasure in sharing, on occasion bringing one or another friend who departed with total depletion from the combined attack.

Alan chanced taking William to Lichfield in the autumn for a visit to some cousins. The two daughters were about William's age and were immediately taken by his looks. One of the girls was falling totally in love with his alert but soft eyes. Because of the giggling girls, those eyes were like those of a doe, showing alarm. On the last day of the visit, with William looking forward to departure, they spent the morning at the market where the girls carried on ceaseless chatter while guiding them from stall to stall.

That morning was a fateful one. William Simpson, the Quaker, had come into the market; as he had gone through the streets he had set the women to screaming and fainting. Alan's cousins stared for quite some time before recovering their senses and entering into appropriate swoons. They crumpled to the ground, wholly forgotten by Alan and William, who were absorbed by the sight. The people seemed to dissolve in making way for Simpson as he dipped over and over into his sack and tossed his money about, crying out, "Lo! A sign of my nakedness! Woe unto the city of Lichfield."

Between his hairy legs, Simpson's loose genitals swung freely with each step. He was a burly man with a large chest; the nipples were surrounded by kinky hair like that over the breastbone. His face was full and he was partially bald. His eyes held a piercing gaze. He was one of many who had taken to giving their "signs" in most of the cities. Men and women had been moved to show signs of their nakedness from their image of God and righteous holiness and knowledge of the way God would strip them bare and naked as thy were. Invariably, they were imprisoned or whipped.

Simpson's "Woe unto the city of Lichfield" echoed the words George Fox had cried out in this same market ten years before, in the cold of winter with his feet unshod. Alan and William let Simpson stride between them, his loud voice almost setting their ears ringing. Even with reality before him, William could not believe he was actually seeing the figure with the straight back, the sagging buttocks—their lower parts covered with curled hair—and the heavy calves.

William set Alan laughing heartily in the carriage on the way back to the manor. He had brought out his genitals while crying, "Lo! A sign of my nakedness! Woe unto you whom I spray with spunk!"

At the house he was worse. By the time Alan left his parents and got up to the chamber, William was striding about the room totally naked, jerking his hips with each step so his erection would thump against his thigh and making the same statements.

"'Tis great effect marked on you by the sight of Simpson, William. What city have you picked for yourself?"

"It struck me, Alan, that had it been you going about in such a way, even the men would have been swooning! Can you imagine what that would be like? With you so truly naked and with pego roared stiff, no one could bear it!"

Alan laughed. "And would you visit me in prison?"

"They could not imprison you."

"'Tis what they could do."

"They could not, because they would be powerless with the sight of you. And if I joined with you, head shaven clean, then they would surely be struck dumb by the sight of doubleness!"

Alan seemed remote and not to be listening as he slipped out of his clothing. William muttered with disappointment: "You have not heard any of what I have said. I set up amusement and you do not laugh."

"William," Alan said, deep in thought, "I have

117

heard every word you said. It has stirred something in me and I know not what."

As he settled into the chair and William approached, Alan said, "No, no… strut about that way but wait. Come here; let me bring you up until you are really stiff, so whatever you might butt will be left with your mark."

While he leaned back and watched the prancing youth, he saw only one who brought his own prick erect. He tried seeing William as others might look at him. He closed his eyes and let his mind visualize the youth, blanking out any hair he had and making him his equal. Startling was hardly the word for it, especially when he saw himself with his powerful body playing the part of lover.

"How long do you keep me pacing?" It sounded like a complaint. "My purse near pushes my things inside me and will empty on the floor!"

Alan opened his eyes partially and sprawled low in the chair, his legs widespread.

"Waste not on the floor—come, make your marks!"

Alan postponed his thinking and opened his arms in welcome invitation, disconcerting William only for the moment when he slipped off the chair to his knees. At the same time William came into reach; the youth was not as primed as he claimed to be and Alan took advantage, letting his throat and tongue case William's urgency upward in steps, halting more and more frequently to let the heavy throbs diminish against his cheek while his tongue urged the testicles to creep higher into the crotch. When the youth's hands began digging into his shoulders, knees flexing and thighs spreading wider with their muscles in bold relief and the throbs were heavier. Alan teased the blunt briefly and then bottomed; his throat strained against the sudden hardness and instantly felt the driving force racing down the shaft, the white heat hurtling deeply.

The gripping at his shoulders, the straining to go deeper, the heavy, continuing throbs in his throat and William's moans heightened Alan's needs. He could not wait, but grabbed his own pulsing cock and brought it up with vibrating hand. William was still trembling as his cock jerked dryly in Alan's throat when his own first hot streak came on in a violent rush.

Gradually, Alan began to connect some matters. For the longest time, William used references to Simpson as a ruse and encouraged Alan to play the part for their amusement, taking advantage of Alan's inevitable erection. He was just as apt to hide in the orchard and, when Alan came to search, drop silently from a branch, directly in Alan's path like a naked specter.

It was William who brought to the stable a visiting cousin a year younger than Alan and also a powerfully built man; on the prearranged pretext of having to fetch Alan, William left. An instant later, Alan dropped from his hiding place into the hay. The cousin froze into immobility: William had given him no description of Alan, and the sudden appearance of a muscular creature with an erection more bold for its lack of hair set him to gulping in terror. Alan acted quickly and found no resistance from the man, as he was toppled into the hay with breeches already settling below his knees. The cousin seemed to have no strength as he automatically tried to defend himself against the man who was straddling his chest. The stifled laugher from behind caused the loss of Alan's penetrating glare and the cousin looked baffled for a moment before shoving Alan from him. But he was still powerless, for William had sneaked in and firmly laid hold of his cousin's genitals.

William dared not let go as his cousin called upon both well-used and rarely employed words to illustrate his displeasure. At last, remembering his exceptional fright, he caught their spirits and fell back on the hay laughing. Subtly, his laughter became soft moans and he reached for Alan. William's cheeks were deeply hollowed as he worked on his cousin's stiffening cock. Under urging, Alan again straddled the barreled chest and let the lips surround his tip while the farm-strengthened hands worked tirelessly. The look came into the cousin's eyes at the same moment William began his own moans; knowing that William and his cousin were both climaxing, Alan burst, vainly trying to keep his cock imprisoned in the choking, sputtering mouth.

The cousin left the stable an hour later, dazed, tired and prone to short bursts of laughter as he recalled his initial fright. He dared not look back to wave farewell, for if Alan had any semblance of an erection, his will would not be strong enough to keeping him from turning back. Alan found revelation rather than amusement in the fact that his sudden display had left a stalwart individual powerless.

"What are you smiling about?" William asked as he and Alan remained sprawled on the hay. "I hope it is not that you find him more pleasant than me."

"No, sweet William, you are my precious one, though I will not mind in the least if you bring him here each day left in his visit. He is versatile and enjoys spunk in or on him as much as we do."

"So that is why you smile?"

"No. I have found the key which may open a door in my mind. Ever since the day we saw Simpson, with all your teasing I have been trying to open this door wherein hides a thought."

William looked puzzled and began running his fingers along Alan's body as he liked doing for hours, if permitted, relishing the skin.

"I cannot follow you—what has given you this key?"

"William, the Spanish Dons are most particular about their manner of dress. They appear to find the body most shameful and they go about, even in the tropics, properly attired in their somber black garb. Never do they even permit a singlet to be open at the chest."

"'Tis a silly thing, seems to me," William replied. "I would love greatly to be where it is always warm and have us be together, always naked. It would please me to be able to see you where I could reach out like this for comfort."

"Now stop, William; let it be—'tis near sore. You and your cousin can excite a man beyond reason. Now stop, lest you be sorry if I set to sucking until you are mad with screaming."

He made a slight movement and William pulled away hurriedly.

"Now, let me examine this matter without—oh, all right. Come here."

William was pouting, but he quickly moved close

121

and cuddled, resting his head on Alan's shoulder and putting his hand back on Alan's crotch.

"Would you like to take me to the tropics with you, Alan? An island with only us upon it would be ideal; we would have nothing to do and could be this close for many hours. I would be your slave and wash you with my tongue twice each day. You could drink of me—"

"William! How can you expect me to think about anything other than pegos and bollocks when you go on this way?" He flinched as William set his fist none-too gently on Alan's abdomen.

"Yes, I would like to promise that I would take you to an island, but I cannot even find the means to take myself there. If I could, I want first to take revenge for the treatment I received. I would like nothing more than to strip those fancy clothes from every Spaniard in Hispaniola and force him to run about naked, cracking a whip across his back if he is not fast enough or if he does not keep himself stiff. It is a sad thing how quick they are with a whip or a cat if one is not to their standards.

"Their black hearts are known to the word through their blasted Inquisition and tortures. It makes it seem better to ram a cutlass into their guts like this!" he exclaimed, as he turned swiftly and pushed his flaccid prick against William's belly.

William broke into wild laughter: "You need to polish your cutlass, else your ramming is most ineffective!"

Alan slapped him for his impertinence, but had to laugh as well. He settled back again and let his eyes take on a dreamy look.

"I see a ship—it would be a private ship. It would be no buccaneer, for no governor would commission one in such deeds as this one would do. This ship would hoist a Jolly Roger at the sight of a Spanish vessel and set chase.

"The crew would be vicious fighters and their comrades would put the vessel adrift. Then comes the moment when grappling irons sail through the air and their ropes and chains go taut. The two ships meet with a loud crash!

"The Dons are well prepared: Their men stand with raised swords and pistols. I would be the first to board, bearing only cutlass held forward at the same stiff angle as my pego!"

He paused for effect and then asked, "Would they be as shattered as the ship about them while our cutlasses spilled their blood and split each in two?"

William was breathing heavily, imagining the scene and caught up in a story of pirates. Then he let out a long sigh and said, "'Twould not be a success."

"But why not?" puzzled Alan.

"You would need me at your side, armed like you—between us, we would give them something to think about!"

Alan pulled him close, full of affection. "You have too much beautiful hair on your head to frighten them." Before William could utter a word, Alan added, "And we'll not be hearing of how you can take care of that!"

Though his dream had been merely that, as time went on Alan found himself dwelling on the dream, and William supported him, adding ridiculous elements which were never obvious until they had been explained. Depending on the mood, he would set William running or yielding for making a farce.

"You speak so often of this pirate matter, Alan," he said one day in a rare serious mood. "Could it be you would do these things?"

"'Tis what I wish, William. I have been four years wanting to revenge myself. Giles was certain this would pass in time—he is most wrong. By all rights one should say insanity has taken me. I have become obsessed with the need."

"Then you should become insane. I swear, you must think you do carry a cutlass for all the ramming my belly has been taking!"

"Have a thoughtlessly hurt you?" Alan was all concern.

"'Twould take a sharper point to bring hurt than any you inflict with your bluntness!" There was a coy twinkle in William's eye. "If this be the trace of insanity, I say you should take insanity on in full. I could revel in it!"

"Now, be serious! I suspect your parents find themselves rid of a pest and I should return them to you so I can think, with no bollock-mad creature distracting me. One of these days I shall be off with a pirate crew and leave you to fend for yourself."

Inside, he wondered if he could get along for any period without William and gazed at him intently.

"I would venture that you would do well with whom you pleased. For your 19 years, you have become strikingly handsome of face and body. Yes, cast those seemingly innocent eyes like that at anyone else and he would fall to his knees before you to taste your sweetness. Your locks beg for roaming hands to disturb them—as I constantly keep them askew—or even to be like a blanket, as when you let me cover my pego.

"Your ears lie so flat, they are like open windows in which one needs to enter like a breeze, their smallness hardly permitting a tongue. Not seeming of muscle, your body yet has the solidity my pego is now acquiring, and if you continue to sit there accepting all this dripping praise, then you deserve to be left here. I would accomplish nothing, but wanting only to suck you until I can reach what can be drawn into my throat to gain my reward!

"I would rather have you suck me, have your lips pass more words. You were saying? About the solidity of my body?"

Alan laughed as he turned on William and flattened him on the hillock beyond the orchard: "You are a vain bastard!"

He buried his face against William's neck and, after he had tasted of the flesh there, lifted his head only enough to say, "But a most adorable bastard!"

When he nibbled on the never-rising nipple, his hands were no less busy searching along the chest. He looked to see that he had left no marks and passed his hand over the wide expanse with firm pressure.

"I am most happy that you are not like your cousin and are so bare. There was a time when I thought I would look forward to a bush of it, but today I am more grateful you have grown little more of a crop than when I first met you." He pulled away, beyond reach. "William, it would please me to see you stand."

Alan poured more praise on the youth, all of it

heartfelt. In his search for points, he flashed memories of Malcolm, Michael and Hallet. The four whom he most adored had one common factor: Though Hallet was by far of a size below what Alan considered average and Malcolm, Michael and William were about what he thought the norm, all of them had genitals which appeared to protrude nobly. If a man becomes naked, the eyes invariably stray to evaluate his assets. With these four, the eyes were forced to look boldly.

"Do you accept me rather than discard me? You have gone into silence?" William asked.

"Accept you for what?" Alan seemed vague with musing.

"As one of your pirates, of course."

Alan was caught off guard. He had been picturing the four and himself at the bulwark of a ship on the verge of boarding one grappled, momentarily to put the other crew into a trance. He quickly looked at the provocative attitude of William, at the cock being smoothly and lovingly stroked.

"You would be a right handsome pirate!" he declared.

"Then let me prove my skill with my trusty cutlass! Prepare to defend yourself. Show your cutlass!" he cried as he fell to Alan's side in reverse position. Their parrying and thrusting began in earnest, with sufficient zest to set strains on the jaws.

Parrying and thrusting with sharp iron came into Alan's life in the spring of 1665: On the 4th of March, England's Charles II had declared war on the Dutch.

Shortly after, Alan received a last letter from Hallet, who felt he could perform a better service by joining the naval forces: "If, as you show in your letters, you still have the madness, you should consider serving your king in that manner to better avail," Giles had written. He had said little more.

Life at the manor was exceedingly dull. Alan had performed his share of the duties there with total lack of interest. Had it not been for William, he would have left long before. As it was, his father had realized this condition and when it came to the time where Alan seemed unable to get enough of William, William's father agreed on permanent residence. It was not a great price to keep a son. But for all of his virility, William could not alleviate the horrendous craving that seemed to be eating through Alan. Even their wordplay of the last two years became a serious matter, for Alan and William bore several scars as reminders that Alan had lost sight when those were inflicted, seeing perhaps a Spaniard rather than his beloved William.

"Give a hand, Alan," William pleaded while Alan had been thinking of Hallet's decision. "My translation of this Latin makes little sense."

Alan stilled the tapping of the letter against his palm and looked over William, who was sprawled across the bed, the book in the ring of light from the candle. It did not seem like mid-day. The sky was gloomy and the wind whistled. There was little anyone could do on a day like that. He seemed to make rising from the chair seem a great effort.

"Does Hallet send bad news?"

Alan was about to sit down on the bed, but William was accustomed to this behavior. He closed his book and waited. At last Alan turned.

127

"Now, will you sit here and tell me?"

"Hallet is going to war with the naval forces," Alan announced as he was about to sit. "They will need surgeons, you know."

William tugged at the sleeve of Alan's singlet until their eyes met. He examined them thoroughly. In a quiet voice he asked, "When are you going?"

Alan took a deep breath and let it out as a sigh. The moment of decision had already passed, even though he had not known until this time.

"As soon as I am able."

"You still have a love for Hallet," William said understandingly.

Alan touched the ruddy cheek, fringed for lack of a shave, and let William's questioning gaze enter into him to see the answer. He also voiced it while William was discovering it.

"I love Hallet. I love Malcolm and Michael too. I love you very dearly, William... you also had a love for Hallet, though your desire for me was stronger. If you were to meet Malcolm and Michael, you would love them too. This was clear to me when we had your cousin and other friends.

"None that I can see changed any of the love we have for each other. While I am gone you will be free and no doubt deeply involved with others. I would venture that a moment alone, if I return, would warrant actions as if no others had been in between."

William's gaze continued searching into Alan. When he withdrew, he closed his eyes and set his head back on his pillows. Even his breathing seemed still for those few moments before he opened his eyes, avoiding looking directly at Alan. His voice was very tight when he said, "I shall be joining you the day you go. Pray that we will be on the same ship."

Alan took William to London with him. They became lowly fighting men under Montague's command. Alan took to naval regimentation as though he had been born into the services. As they cruised off Texel, in May, he was already several echelons above William and was fired with great ambition to get to the top. It was also in that same month that William received orders for transfer to another vessel.

Alan had been severely chastised for the behavior the two displayed with their obvious affection for each other. Nevertheless, Alan's superior officer did permit several hours of privacy in his cabin for their farewell.

Two days later, Alan learned why when he was invited to the same cabin. His open accusation was buffeted about until the officer tired of the game.

"It would be most simple to demote you," he informed Alan. "One step at a time for each refusal!"

Alan's eyes flashed... then, with a clatter, he dropped his belt and began undoing his jacket.

Alan brought every technique he had ever uncovered into play. When the officer begged him to be raised to a climax, Alan reached for the pomade. His eyes stayed on the reared buttocks—which bristled with hair that appeared to stand on end with as much anticipation as the officer showed. Desire for this form of entry had left Alan completely after the damage he had sustained in Barbados, and although William had felt capable Alan never wished to enter anyone again, well aware that he could easily bring the same painful experience to them. At this moment, in his eyes, the officer, the Wilsons and the Spaniards were in the same category.

He gave little heed when the officer began struggling and Alan tightened his arms about him until he had completed the steady drive which finally had his solid abdomen pressing the buttocks flat. He went easy in his succeeding movements until the officer who had been at such a pitch suddenly tightened; Alan could sense every burst filtering between the linens and the tangle on the officer's belly. He angled slightly and continued his easy motion, closing his ears to the pleas; the officer sounded as though he were choking as he added to the spoiling. When he was crying out that he could take no more, Alan shifted to achieve his own satisfaction. He closed his eyes and pictured his arms around William during one of their modes of play, with William's belly already slicked by his own coming and Alan viciously pounding away, knowing he could do the youth no hurt. The officer's cries could have been off in the orchard for all Alan cared.

The first letter with the interchange of messages between vessels sent Alan into a rage. It was bad enough to learn that William had been transferred to the ship carrying Hallet, but he had also found out that the transfer had been a conspiracy between four of the officers. Several times a week, officers became incapacitated with bum afflictions, to the consternation of the surgeon aboard. But Alan also began receiving his promotions; it was simple—either sign the request or be split.

Alan received a commendation for his valor and ingenuity when the forces moved on the Dutch merchant fleet. When they withdrew, 150 of the ships had been blown up or set afire. In actuality, this was a small percentage when set against the total of over

10,000 ships the Dutch had on the waters that year, but the destruction of even a single ship counted. Alan was stepped up rapidly and the officers who had used him found themselves in the position where Alan invited them to *his* cabin, and woe to the one who did not bring his own pomade. The fear of this command had them combine forces once more. Montague was highly confused by their request for one William Mead to be transferred back.

Alan, William and Hallet, however, found themselves to be compatible drinkers in a tavern in the spring of 1667. The fleet had been recalled and was laid up at the Chatham docks. With nothing better to do, they caroused in the tavern through the evening and then in the room they had hired. There was no partiality between them and they brought no one along unless all three showed interest.

They did not join in the jeering with the rest of the men on the 22nd of June, when the Dutch fleet had sailed in and took by surprise the ill-manned fleet so openly laid up. It was a sad sight to see the destruction while they were powerless ashore. The worst was to see the capture of the Royal Charles and to have the Dutch sail it off. Alan put his arms over the shoulders of Hallet and William and drew them both close. Their naval careers had finished.

Chapter Twelve

"Have you not yet had enough of killing and destruction in the war?" asked Hallet, astounded by Alan's decision.

A restlessness developed within a week after the three took quarters in London. William was no better, patterning himself after his idol. Now in his 22nd year and past showing any childish traits, he had exceeded his mentor and could very well select those whom he wished to favor. Like Alan, he issued tirades against the injustices of the Wilson family and their kind, along with the Spaniards and now the Dutch. In some odd way, Alan had put it into William's head that the previous year's Great Fire of London was arson committed by the Dutch, which thereby justified adding them to the list. There were only the French left without accusation.

"This would not be like a war!" countered William. "Can you not see that this would be a pirate ship?"

"Though the weight be smaller, William, it is still war," Alan replied. "I want nothing to do with this."

Alan poured out convincing arguments for why they needed a good surgeon like Hallet aboard the ship. All the while, Hallet watched William closely. He was behind Alan's chair, leaning so his cheek rested on Alan's pate, and he was slowly moving the arm he had buried inside Alan's singlet. Hallet's fingertips could almost feel the smooth skin he never tired of touching. He felt he could not blame him, but Alan and William were insatiable in their need for constant contact and thereby exaggerated demands on sexual prowess. In their mutual quest for satisfaction, they had had become increasingly rough—especially when their resources were scant.

They had taken to having William supine on the high bed, his head tilted over the side with Alan there, feet planted on the floor and Alan's body at a slight angle over William and his buttocks straining while he rammed his full length in and out of William's gullet, his overtaxed testicles thudding against the youth's eyelids. William would writhe on the bed, pleasuring more if the violence raised muscles like intertwined cables on Alan's thighs. In his ecstasy, the veins of William's rigid cock bulged dark blue under the light-colored skin and the cockhead was bold with color. The sight in front of Alan's eyes and the youth's hands gliding up and down his body would finally bring him to a crashing climax. With the approach of it, William would pass one hand down to forcefully whip further redness into his prick and, after Alan's last slam, William's body would convulse while a few drops would trickle down his thumb.

"...and besides," Alan said, "we need you, Hallet, not to engage in fighting, but for your body. Your pego and bollocks be commanding—can you not consider it? 'Tis enough of a great difficulty we will have finding a willing and remarkable crew to fill my needs as I see them."

They undoubtedly would, Hallet told himself.

The madness of the scheme had an intrigue for him, even though he wanted no part of it. Having reached the age of 35 and being tired of the gory sights of battle, Hallet's inclination had been to settle in a thriving community and set up practice. He could be very happy that way with a mate. And yet…

"You and your bloody pirate ship!" His exclamation was muffled. He watched the triumphant smile beginning to develop on Alan's parted lips. The exposure of strong white teeth had increased perceptibly. "How can I settle in a hamlet knowing you have a sporting ship and a tempting, naked crew!" He cautioned Alan with a raised finger. "Do not smile so broadly until you hear my conditions."

"Any—name them!" Alan was eager.

"I wish an assistant. He is one who was with me during the war and one I had hoped to keep under my charm and happy with life in a hamlet, even though he be little older than William and craves London and the city life."

"If you say he meets most of the requirements, I would be highly pleased to have two surgeons aboard."

"Oh, I am certain that he exceeds your needs," Hallet said with a smug look. "Naturally, like most surgeons, he has no great build. I find him good of face, though you have no requirements on that score. When stark, his body stands out because his legs are somewhat dark with hair, but he is bare from the navel upward. You would find him with excessive crop, but you said this was not of great importance as long as the prick and purse are most apparent."

Hallet looked as though he were about to divulge one of the great secrets of his life.

"Alan, his prick is most narrow next to yours, perhaps more like William's. Yet when hanging it is as long as yours in erection!"

Alan looked at him accusingly: "You bloody old bugger!"

Alan could hear William choking back laughter and turned his head up.

"William?" he asked.

"He made me swear I would never tell you about Russell—so help me! Now that 'tis out, I can only say that you should see him in stiffness! 'Tis unbelievable."

Alan did not have to ask—William had most certainly tasted Russell.

"Granted!" he told Hallet. "I accept that condition. Are there more?"

"We shall take passage with you and serve you well, but there will come a time when we have had our fill. You will release us upon our notification."

"I could be left without any surgeons in that case," Alan declared and fell to thinking. Hallet remained silent, to show he was immovable on that point. "Well," Alan finally announced, "It seems I have little choice. I would hope we have some luck in locating another surgeon before you make such a decision. Are there more such awkward conditions?"

"That is the last of them, except that I must assume beyond any doubt that you will set yourself on my friend and you should permit me opportunity for gratification, taking on whoever pleases me."

Alan rose quickly from his chair and William's arm, caught within, ripped the singlet.

"Pay no heed, William," said Alan, slipping it off. "We seal our bargain with Hallet on this spot. His

135

thoughts of a naked crew have had him squirming for some time now and he needs relief."

"No, Alan!" Hallet cried, but his utterance was not convincing. As William began yanking off the singlet, Hallet raised his arms with weak threats, He had not been part of their sport in some days and he relished the attack. More and more, he had been thinking about penetrating William curled in his customary fetal position against Alan, with William masturbating while Alan's cock strove to fill Hallet's depths.

"William," Alan declared as he threw his arm over the youth's shoulder while they walked up the street to the inn, "This visit to Woolrich could not have been better timed. I am filled with joy this moment."

"'Tis my feeling too," he responded, linking his arm over Alan's.

The transaction concluded with one Phineus Pett was bringing Alan's dream closer to reality. Pett originally had given Alan quite a setback when he estimated the cost of a vessel to Alan's specifications: Without guns, supplies small arms and other necessities, Alan would have been barely able to cover the cost from the money he had obtained through sale of the manor. When his parents had died of the plague in 1665, after the residents of London fled the city and carried the pestilence in their belongings, Alan ordered the sale immediately with no desire to ever again see the place. But Pett was demanding nearly every pound: When they began compromising on features, Alan became unhappy, for he was getting nothing better than a merchantman vessel. In the last two days, Pett had spent little time with Alan. He was distracted primarily by calls for his presence in London to consult on the rebuilding of the naval fleet the Dutch had destroyed.

The vision of profits made Pett generous at a weak moment and he showed Alan a vessel which had been under construction for a firm that had gone into bankruptcy. The more important factors—the ones which would give speed and maneuverability—were to be included and the vessel would be nearly what Alan wanted in the first place and within his budget. Pett turned details over to his son, Peter, who began modifying their drafter plans for the ship.

When Peter had entered the last of the details on the plan and the work was to proceed, William and Alan returned to London. There they found that Hallet had located his friend, Russell Stock, and that the young fellow took to the pirate plan like any youth seeking adventure. He had reservations about the nudity, since he was propositioned upon the slightest exposure, but the compliments Alan tossed out about the attractiveness of a long cock made him relent.

Russell's frame was narrow and he was about an inch taller than Hallet, but this only exaggerated his predominant feature. Below a crop lush enough and sufficiently lengthy to bear a comb were encased small testicles which rode forward and over them, like the long end of a rope, draped a desirable cock. Hallet was wrong: The narrowness he claimed was a deception brought by the length—Russell was more than qualified. Alan took a quick glance at Hallet; the look was there—Hallet needed more time with Russell. Alan would learn the length under erection later.

Alan conscientiously tried to advance his plans for

the vessel in London, but came to realize that his knowledge about ships—though gained with the naval forces—was not extensive. He had to get officers with experience to assist him. He considered Bristol to be the best location for that endeavor and so he and William took rooms there, separate in case of the eventuality that more than one prospects was at hand. Their search seemed to uncover only ordinary seamen, though some were extraordinarily endowed with semen.

There was one particular evening when they were about to dine at the inn, that a man came in. He ordered a tankard of ale and then leaned on the bar as he looked about. Alan had noticed him the instant he entered from the street and found his heart racing. There could be no doubt but that the officer in the thick blue coat with brass buttons was none other than Malcolm Lowe. No one else could possibly lean in that provocative fashion, seeming to hinge back from the hips far enough to have the open coat hang straight down from his shoulders and rest inches behind his buttocks.

Malcolm wore his 31 years well. His features had hardened somewhat, yet they retained a boyish charm. His eyes were more penetration in their gaze, and they rested lightly on Alan before scanning the room. Again, they came to rest on Alan: They had acquired a slight squint in their defense against the brightly sunlit sea. Below them, the mouth seemed fuller than Alan ever remembered it, the lips red with glowing sensuality.

Malcolm sauntered to the table when Alan beckoned, but appeared stunned to learn that this was the Alan he had known.

"I well remember you," he said, his eyes giving a momentary flash. "But I would not have recognized you. You were such a tall, thin thing and now you look so huge in that fancy doublet. The periwig does you little, justice, I must say." He paused and his eyes flickered. "Alan," he concluded, "you are admirably different."

Malcolm was as completely at ease and relaxed as Alan had ever seen him. He accepted their invitation to dine without hesitation. From then, Alan found it difficult to concentrate with such handsome features always focused on him, especially when the fires danced in Malcolm's eyes during his recounting of adventures while serving under French pirate *L'Ollonaise*. Malcolm had escaped form the plantation where he had been indentured by killing the overseer and rousing the others to rebellion. With luck in stowing away, he made his way to Tortuga and there joined the *filibustiers*. His close attentions to his master helped him scale himself upward; he learned the navigation and the art of sailing, finally becoming the ship's master's mate.

Malcolm's tales of *L'Ollonaise*'s atrocities were not fit for the dinner table and William slowed his eating when Malcolm described with zeal how *L'Ollonaise* would have a man's stomach slit if ransom was slow in coming, just enough to permit pulling out a length of his entrails which could be fastened to a post. He would then be set to dancing about by thrusting firebrands against his buttocks and genitals until he had danced away as far as the entire length of his entrails would permit. His tale of how *L'Ollonaise* would tear out a living man's heart made William wonder if he would ever eat again.

"My story is not as exciting as yours," Alan confessed, "though it had me near death several times."

"Morgan said he found you in Santa Jago. I was most distressed when I learned I had missed you—you had returned to England. Perhaps that was when I began to feel a need for cold weather and the look of England instead of the tropics.

"I have just come off the ship and already I know that I have no need for cold weather. But you, do you wish to return there? Seeing you again, finding you looking so virile, I know my pleasure would be complete and I would return with you at my side."

"There is much to discuss, Malcolm. I thank you for saying you find pleasure with me—from that day in the hold, you have often been in my thoughts."

"I can see you need to be on your own this night," William whispered in Alan's ear. "I know not why, but I be neutral toward you at this time, though with a happiness for you. I shall see if I can find my pleasure at the Turtleback Tavern." William smiled as Alan nodded vaguely.

Neither he nor Malcolm noticed William's departure, continuing their gazes at each other. Alan caught up with the elusive flickering of flames in the dark eyes at the other side of the table. He could no longer concentrate on Malcolm's words and suggested that they seek quiet in his room. They entered bearing three bottles of ale apiece to sustain them through Alan's long story, which Malcolm insisted on hearing. Alan began it by doffing his wig.

Malcolm's lips, still never seeming to achieve a full smile, lifted enough at the corners to show that he was indeed smiling.

"I have not seen one so bald," he said. "I venture that it is more to my liking than that blasted wig you wear."

Relieved by that beginning, Alan launched into his story and when he reached the fatal day of discovering what had taken place form infection, Malcolm said, having misunderstood the implications, "But most men grow bald, Alan." He ran his fingers through his own thick locks and said, "I think not I— there is too much."

Alan stripped off his doublet and then the singlet, extending his arms.

Malcolm let his lips part; lightly, he passed his tongue over as though they had gone dry.

"Triced at the mast, I always found your thin frame exciting. I would give a fortune to see you there now." He squinted. "I thought I had done well, but my chest is nowhere near as heavy as yours." More of a smile formed. "At that time, sucking a crewman or letting him take a bit of brown was in the line of duty. I used to bite my tongue to keep from falling on my knees before you, to clutch at the heavy hair which I envied you having and to take every drop he beat out of you. No, don't be so surprised. You may not remember how I used to sleep close by you and how I once raised my courage to at least take hold of you."

"I have never forgotten that, Malcolm, but in my desire to have you it had never entered my mind that perhaps you wanted me." Alan grunted and laughed softly. "To think I had been planning entrapment for you—need I force more?"

Malcolm peered from under his brows and pulled the tie of his singlet. As the flaps parted, a patch of curly black hair was exposed, bold in the expanse of his broad chest.

"Wait!" Alan ordered. "My singlet was removed so you might appraise how devoid of hair I have become, thanks to the bastards. But you make me recall that perhaps I had none, or very little, when we first me. Sixteen years make one forget such details."

"Elsewhere as well?" Malcolm asked.

"Every bit, and I shall show you."

When Alan stood wholly naked, Malcolm's eyes missed not a detail. He ended his scrutiny by saying, "I had forgotten how massive you were," and began pulling off his singlet.

Naked and erect, they stood apart, their bodies in stark contrast before the dancing candles flame—Alan's smooth flesh seemed not to reflect the light but rather to glow translucently from some inner ember, while the curly black hairs that matted Malcolm's body from throat to ankles diffused the glare into infinitesimal slivers that shimmered like a fine, silvery cloak. Distinct from the soft lights of their forms was the conflagration of passion that blazed in their eyes, brighter even than the Great Fire of London.

Like two luminous specters they floated together, touching, then fusing into a single molten entity. Spearing tongues, flitting hands and passionate memories of his long-lost love brought Alan to a quick peak, his quiveringly rigid cock erupted in hot gushes of spunk that splattered on Malcolm's belly and caught on the fine hair like white droplets on a silky spider web.

A waft of night air cooled their bodies as they hesitantly parted. Gazing into Malcolm's still burning eyes, Alan realized that his search had ended, that anything which might occur in the future would be anticlimactic to this reunion of mind, spirit and body.

Malcolm had been the prime motivator, the igniter of Alan's flaming obsession with revenge against those who had torn them apart, he thought as he sank to his knees and grasped his lover's trembling pego. His lips compressed around the trembling knob, his tongue flicked into the tiny slit and his mind obliterated all thoughts of violence and vengeance. Gone were the loneliness, the uncertainty and ambivalence that had plagued his very existence since they had parted as youths 16 long years before. Now his life was full.

Whatever the future held, Alan thought, gently squeezing Malcolm's pulsing bollocks, they would face it together in their own paradise, oblivious to consternation. As if to provide liquor to toast that pledge, Malcolm's cock jerked mightily. Alan felt a surging heat pas his osculating lips and when it spewed into his mouth, he drank deeply of the heady wine of love.

TO BE CONTINUED...

In *Naked Launch, Book Two*, the further adventures of Alan Steele

About 120 Days

120 Days is an imprint of Riverdale Avenue Books dedicated to reprinting classic erotica, especially the LGBT titles of the late 20th Century. These vintage gay erotic novels, many written by novelists unable to find other outlets for fiction about gay men and women, peaked between 1968 and 1982. As censorship laws were struck down across the US, the best of these writers continued to turn out well-plotted genre novels—spy thrillers, science-fiction tales, mysteries, swashbuckling adventures, gothic romances and even pre-"Brokeback Mountain" westerns— within whose conventions they were able to explore the full range of their characters' lives. Surprisingly modern with just a dash of retro appeal these largely-forgotten novels are both great, fun reads and a bracing reminder that times change but people don't.

Other Riverdale Avenue Books Titles You Might Enjoy

Man Eater
by Dick Jones

Vampire's Kiss
By Sonny Barker

A Gay Thing Happened on the Way to the Forum
By Bert Shrader

Three Ring Circus
By John Maggie

Night of the Sadist
By Paul Laurie

Fangsters: Clan of the Jersey Boys
By Ryan Field

Fangsters 2: Gangbang Fangsters
By Ryan Field

Valley of the Dudes
By Ryan Field

Stepbrothers in the Attic
By Ryan Field

50 Shades of Gay
By Jeffery Self

The Hunger Gays
By Nathan Alexander

You Must Remember This
By John Michael Curlovich

www.ingramcontent.com/pod-product-compliance
Lightning Source LLC
Chambersburg PA
CBHW071438260626
47170CB00008B/2760